SECOND
CHANCES

SEC⊕ND
CHANCES

a Novel by
WILLIAM D. MECHAM

atmosphere press

Chapter 1

Lying in the hospital bed, I took time to reflect on my life. I'd been so busy trying to get rich in the last sixty-odd years that I hadn't thought about where I'd been and where I'd go next. Fredrick Lloyd Lambson—that's me—had ambitions but failed to plan too far in advance and sometimes took shortcuts rather than put in the effort. It wasn't a bad life, and I made a decent living, invested well, and accumulated a fair sum, but in the back of my mind, I felt I could have done better! While chasing the almighty dollar, I'd trashed my body by neglecting it. Too much good living and not enough exercise had led me to obesity, diabetes, and heart disease. I was a walking co-morbidity clinic, and it was literally killing me. My heart was giving out, my kidneys were shot, and I had a *fatty* liver. Having been told I had a short time to live, it grieved me to be tallying my regrets. I wondered what I could have done differently if I could do it over again.

I was thinking this when the psychologist came into my room. He didn't tell me he was a psychologist. He just came in, introducing himself as Dr. Randquist, and inquired about how I felt, and asked if I was being treated okay. As we talked, he managed to drag my life story out of me since I tend to be gregarious. At that moment, I preferred talking to a stranger rather than one of my family, who would construe my mood as morose and depressed. I didn't think I was depressed, just introspective! Soon, we got down to facts.

"So, Mr. Lambson, tell me a little about some of these regrets?"

"Well, to start with, I could've been more successful, if I'd not just coasted along, and let things happen! I should've driven myself to get a degree, and *really* make something of myself—" The doctor interrupted:

"According to what I see, you've been quite successful, business-wise," but I continued:

"I think I could've been better with my family, and especially with my marriage. I've *supported* a family, but my wife *raised* them! I have grandkids but hardly know them. My kids are loving toward me, and respect me for the most part, but I feel I could have been a better father. My wife and I, drifted apart after the kids left home, so we finally divorced. I'm sure I wasn't easy to live with, and she deserves her alimony. Sure, I met their material needs, but I'm just not happy with the way I lived my life!"

"So, tell me a little more about your feelings of failure," the doctor intoned.

"Here's an example: when I was a teenager, I wanted to play a guitar. I even had a guitar given to me, but I lacked the '*stick-to-it-ness*' to learn and practice. I lacked the discipline. So... I never became skilled at playing the guitar!"

"I believe that's quite common in young people. What else?" He asked.

"When it came to secondary education, I went with the flow. I coasted through high school, earning good grades without applying myself too much. When it was time for college, I hadn't put anything aside to pay tuition, nor applied for any scholarships. I had the grades, and I passed the college entrance exams, but I couldn't register because I had no money. As an unskilled person, any job I got to support myself, would lock me into a dead-end job and I'd never get out, so I joined the military.

"I was fortunate they trained me in electronics. This training, and the subsequent long-term experience I gained, shaped my future. Like I said, I went the path of least resistance. I ended up in aerospace and spent my life working in that field. I was deemed a "home-grown engineer," which meant I had the knowledge and experience to do the job, but without a diploma, advancement was impossible. I'd once been told by a senior engineer: 'A degree isn't always needed, but they'll always hold it against you if you don't have one.' So, I hit the career ceiling," I summed up.

"It sounds like you did well without a diploma, but you don't feel satisfied with your accomplishments?"

"Tell me, doc: do you like your job?" I asked out of the blue.

"Why, yes, I do enjoy it, and derive great pleasure from helping people," he answered.

"Uh huh. And where would you be if you hadn't gone to medical school and gotten your diploma? Do you think you'd be happy with whatever you'd ended up doing, without your degree?" I countered.

"Hmmm. I see what you mean, Mr. Lambson. But there are many professions people are happy with, which do not require a college degree," he said resolutely.

"Yes, and a plumber probably makes as much as I did, but I just think I could have done better. If I could have advanced further, I may have been able to do more for my family. So, I should have worked for a degree. I failed in 'due diligence' for my life," I groused.

After an hour of quietly talking to the doctor, I sensed he was looking for something from me. Point blank, he asked: "Mr. Lambson, do you *really* want a chance to do it over?"

"Do you mean regaining my health and going on with my life?" I queried. "It's too late to earn a degree, and make it work. So, I'd still be stuck with the hand I've dealt myself?"

"No," he retorted, "if you had a chance to start, not at the very beginning as a baby, but at a point in life where you could make changes to alter the outcome, so it would be more to your liking, would you take the chance?" he questioned.

Being a person prone to making up scenarios and playing them out in my mind, I was game! "That would be a great opportunity! I really wish I had the option," I said, thinking it was just rhetorical.

"Hold that thought!" The doctor replied, then he rose and left.

Now, what was all that about? Maybe he wanted to get another *shrink* to witness me saying the same thing, and then they'd draw up papers making me "certifiable," turning decision making over to my oldest child! He was gone for quite a while. I guessed all the other *head* doctors were on the golf course. I figured I'd just do some daydreaming, to while away the time until one of my kids showed up. I ended up dozing off.

Being gently awakened by the nurse, I cleared my vision and saw the doc looking on. By this, I mean I saw my primary care physician. Beside him was the psychologist, who I remembered was called Dr. Randquist. My doctor, Dr. Sweeney, smiled and asked:

"Are you alert, Fred? Could you answer some questions?"

"Sure! Fire away," I told them.

"Fred, I've been pretty frank about your prognosis. I told you I didn't expect you to live more than a week if you stayed in the hospital. Probably less if you were discharged. Your body is plain worn out!"

"Sure, doc! I heard you, and I understand! Like the old saying goes: 'If I'd known I was going to live so long, I would've taken better care of my body!' Still, seventy-two isn't a bad age! What's up?" It was at this point I found out Dr. Randquist was a neurologist, not a psychologist. Dr. Sweeney began:

"Dr. Randquist and I have been doing joint research into longevity and neurological disorders associated with various types of traumas. We've experimented with mental acuity and how the brain stores the acquired intelligence of an individual. We believe the brain is a storage medium, like a computer hard drive. We haven't discovered how to download someone's brain storage and play it back, like a flash drive can be read from one computer to another. We do believe, however, if we could transfer the "data" impulses from one brain to another, the second brain would be able to decipher those impulses. As you may gather, the opportunity for such experimentation is limited—" I broke in,

"Doc, you need a guinea pig so you can experiment! I don't think my body would hold out long enough to be of much good to you. So, I don't know how I can help." My doctor continued:

"Fred, your body is failing more each day, but you still possess one of the sharpest minds for your age that I've come across! Normally, with advanced conditions that you manifest, the patient is usually suffering from forms of dementia, but we don't see that in you. Given we have such limited opportunities to further our experimentation, the planets seemed to have aligned, with your failing body and lucid mind, and another subject with complementary properties being available to us at the same time. We believe you're a prime candidate."

"Thanks, doc! But I don't see—" Dr. Randquist took his turn:

"Mr. Lambson, what Dr. Sweeney is trying to say, is we would like your permission to attempt to transfer your intelligence to another brain, to see if the body that brain resides in will be able to function, utilizing your intellect!"

"Do you mean a brain transplant?" I conjectured.

"No, not *per se*, but much the same thing, except there would be no surgery involved. It would equate to a 'data dump' of sorts," Dr. Randquist corrected.

"Gee, that's all very interesting, but last time I checked I had neither a USB nor an RS-232 port anywhere on my body!" I quipped, but Dr. Randquist continued:

"It's not quite like that, Fred. We've developed a probe we can attach to the base of your brain stem. This probe, we believe, can act as a shunt for your thought patterns and memories, to allow them to be sent to another medium of the same type: namely another brain. We believe we can drain, or copy, the essence of a person's intellect, from one storage cell—the brain—and place it in another of the same type. Because it amounts to electrical impulses, there are none of the problems normally associated with transplanting human tissue, such as organ rejection and blood/tissue incompatibility," Dr. Randquist explained.

"Okay! So, let's say I agree. How do we get my family to accept the 'new me' as '*me*'?" Dr. Sweeney chimed in:

"Uh, that's a major sticking point, Fred! If we attempted this and it worked, your family can never know! This type of experimentation is science fiction and skirts the borders of ethics. In this case, let's say it's a new type of 'Witness Protection Program.' Who would believe it, anyway?"

"True," I said, "but that means I'd get a new body, but I couldn't see my loved ones again. That hardly seems fair!" Dr. Randquist jumped back in:

"But Mr. Lambson, if you went right back to being a part of your same old life, what would you be changing? You'd most likely fall back into the same old patterns. It would be like us finding a way to repair your present body and letting you live your same old life, with all those regrets you told me about! This would be your chance to start with almost a clean slate!"

"Okay, I see your point. It's just one of the things I'd have to deal with." I admitted. "Tell me, what age are we talking about dropping me into? I hope it's not too young. As much as going through puberty again appeals to me, it was tough dealing with the hormone overload. And we're talking about me starting again, in the present: there's no time travel involved, right?" Both doctors chuckled.

"No. No time travel. You'd have to deal with this day and age. We're talking about you moving into a body that is twenty-six, chronologically and physically." Excitedly, I said:

"Twenty-six? That's a great age, if I remember correctly! What about his, uh it is a 'him,' right? What about this person's family? How are we going to deal with that?"

"Yes. It's a male, and as far as we've been able to discover, he has no family. He was in the military, and his record indicates no next of kin. Since his discharge, he's been attending college on his G.I. Bill entitlements," Dr. Sweeney informed me.

"So, what's his story? Am I going to have to share his brain with him?" I asked.

Dr. Randquist began reading from a chart:

"His name is William Clay Hollister. He was born in Minnetonka, Minnesota. He was an orphan and spent his formative years in foster homes. He has a sealed juvenile record, so we don't know what he was into as a teen, but he has no record as an adult, and he earned an honorable discharge from the Navy."

"Well, he can't be all that bad if he was a sailor!" I chuckled. "How come he's a candidate for this experiment?"

"He was struck by lightning and is brain dead! We've found no physical damage beyond entry and exit wounds. His reflexes seem to be unimpaired. Although there seems to be no brain wave activity, we've experimented with inserting random pulses into his brain, and the results have been positive. We put the probe on him and tried to 'erase' any remaining impulses, so we don't think you'll have to deal with any residual intellect and memories," Dr. Randquist volunteered.

"So, let me get all this tied up into a neat bundle, to check my understanding. One: you will drain my brain, maybe making *me* brain dead, which means my family will take my tired old body and bury it. You will be essentially taking a couple days off my present existence. Two: If it works, my 'intellect' will awaken in another body, hopefully, and I will be starting off on another life, but an anonymous one, as far as my present family and friends are concerned. Three: I will be free to either repeat my original mistakes in life, or I will be smarter this time, and make a better life, with hopefully less regrets. Is that it, in a nutshell?"

"Mr. Lambson, you've pretty much boiled it down to its pure essence," Dr. Randquist remarked. "The only thing I should add here is that there will be a period of adjustment between your intelligence and your new body. You will almost certainly have to learn to walk and talk again. It may be frustrating for you, at first, because your mind will tell you that you can do it all, but the impulses will have to be matched to your new physical being. We'll keep you here for rehabilitation, just as we would for someone who had been struck by lightning or had any of hundreds of traumatic happenings. Once you're able to get around on your own, we request you return to us regularly so we can keep tabs on your progress and document any anomalies which may arise from the transfer from one body to another. Beyond that, you will be free to live your life, without restrictions from us. In terms of experimentation, it is best to let you have your head, and not restrict you. You won't be a *hot-house flower*. If you experience any strange manifestations, then we request you contact us immediately."

"I must be crazy for even contemplating this, but it seems like an opportunity I can't pass up! Where do I sign?" I said excitedly. Dr. Sweeney answered.

"Actually, the only thing you'll sign is a permission form to allow us access to your body for twenty-four hours after your... uh... demise. This will allow us to remove any evidence of our tampering. It's a mere formality, as bodies are not always immediately claimed by the funeral homes. I hope this line of conversation is not overly morbid?"

"Not at all! Hell, you're offering me a chance to maybe beat the grim reaper. What have I got to bitch about? If it doesn't work, I'll never know! If it works, then you'll have a prize specimen to study." I effused, then added: "This may be the wrong time for me to bring this up, but does this other guy, Bill Hollister, have any money?" Dr. Randquist informed me:

"An insurance company is paying for his recovery, but as part of the hospital's policy, we have a financial statement which says he is at least solvent. He rents an apartment and has an older, paid-for car. He has no credit card debt, which is surprising, but he has credit cards. His savings account has a little over a thousand dollars in it."

"So, when do you plan on doing the... uh... procedure?" I enquired. Dr. Sweeney said:

"At the present, your condition is stable, but it could begin deteriorating at any time. Right now, we'd like to schedule the transfer for tomorrow evening, after visiting hours are over. Would that be convenient for you?"

"It sounds fine to me. That will give me a chance to say my goodbyes. I hope my upbeat demeanor won't make my family suspicious. I can also arrange to make a philanthropic donation to a poor, unfortunate man who was struck by lightning and has no family. I don't think my kids will begrudge me this last splurge. My insurance will more than compensate them for what will be missing from my savings account," I said enthusiastically.

"You're just as sharp and astute as I thought you were. Imagine: feathering your future nest! I hope you're going to be generous, but not too generous. It doesn't pay to arouse suspicions," cautioned Dr. Sweeney.

"Don't worry! I'll make it sound like the final giving

attitude of a sane person and not the raving of some *out-of-his-gourd* lunatic. I need Bill Hollister's savings account number." Dr. Randquist answered me:

"I have it here. I'll write it down for you. Please don't overtax yourself. Get your rest, or you could start the decline sooner than expected."

"Not to worry, doc! I'll be careful. I just want to make a call to my accountant to start the ball rolling. Then, I imagine some of my kids will visit after dinner. I hope they give me something different for dinner tonight. Last night, the soup tasted like dirty dish water!" I groused.

"I'll tell the kitchen to make it taste like 'clean' dish water!" Dr. Sweeney said, smiling.

"Thanks a lot, doc! You bum!" I grinned so he'd know I was kidding.

Talk about a strange turn of events! A couple hours ago, I was bemoaning my lot in life, and looking to just drop into a hole and pull the sod over me! Now, I had expectations of renewing my life, albeit starting from scratch. My mind began spinning, thinking about all the possible pitfalls of taking over someone else's body and life. I'm glad I'd have the guy's I.D. and his fingerprints. I could always cover up my lack of knowledge about such things as PINs and phone numbers and names of people he knew around town. Being struck by lightning would be well-documented and would explain a lot of those situations. People who knew the old Bill Hollister would be saying: 'Poor Bill! I'm so sorry!' I gathered he had had no visitors, so he may not have many friends. Or maybe no one knew about his condition. If what the doctors said was true, my 'rehab' for my new body would also be explained by the *shocking* experience I had! Oh, yeah: I hope he's not ugly!

My accountant was glad to hear from me, I think, but you could tell he hadn't expected to. I gave him directions to donate ten thousand dollars to the account of the unfortunate

Mr. Hollister. Since I, Fredrick Lambson, wouldn't be around for next tax season, I didn't care whether it was a tax-deductible donation or not! I just wanted it well documented so Bill Hollister wouldn't have any trouble with the IRS. I also directed him to give a grant to Drs. Sweeney and Randquist to 'further their research.' You may ask how I can afford to throw all this money around if I thought I was such a failure. Although I was not a degreed engineer, the jobs I had been doing before retirement allowed me to draw a salary 'near' that of a degreed engineer, due to labor laws. I had always saved through the company saving plan, which paid a decent percentage of interest, and I had earned a pension. Using this capital, I had invested it in money market funds, which at the time were doing well. I was not a millionaire, but I could have lived very comfortably for the rest of my life. Now, it would all go to my heirs. My ex-wife would have 'survivors' benefits' to see her through.

During visiting hours that night, I was visited by all my children and grandchildren. Since I was on death's door, but not contagious or overly frail, the hospital waived their normal age restrictions for children. It was a solemn event for them, though the grandchildren were not aware of what was going on. I expressed my love to them all, and although I had secret knowledge, it didn't make me feel any better about not being able to show my love to them, as Bill Hollister. Not for a moment did I have any doubt I would be *reincarnated*! I refused to see it any other way. I made one plea to them:

"Look, guys, downstairs is a poor guy named Bill Hollister. He was struck by a bolt out of the blue! He was a student at the college, and he was struck coming out of the library. He's in bad shape but should pull through. I donated to his bank account, to help him, when he recovers."

I saw a few looks of resentment.

"Come on. With my insurance payout, you won't miss the

piddling few bucks I gave the poor guy. After all, Mr. Hollister is a veteran. Please try to keep track of his progress, and maybe when he's recovered, one of you could visit him and tell him about the old guy who enriched his life a little."

Not getting many positive responses, I just dropped it. Knowing I'd have at least one more visiting session with them, I tried not being maudlin.

Early the next day, my doctors came in and we had a long, quiet conference. Going over the exact procedure, they then gave me a chance to ask my questions. They were not surprised I had so many.

"This procedure is not like buying a new car," I intoned. "Or in this case, a 'used' car, er, uh, I mean body! I won't have a chance to take it for a test drive, so it falls into the category of a *gift horse*, and I shouldn't want to investigate its mouth!" I finished.

"A very astute analogy, Fred!" Dr. Sweeney remarked.

My logical mind, from somewhere in the back kept screaming at me: 'What if it fails?' The emotional part of my mind kept swatting at the back part and telling it to shut up, because if it failed, I'd never know about it, and I would be dead in a couple days anyway if I chickened out and turned down the *new residence*! All in all, while I listened to the Sweeney/Randquist duet, my mind was working like mad, trying to capture it all; digest it; and keep from calling it off!

Even before visiting hours, my oldest son, Stephen, came charging in.

"Did you know the 'poor Mr. Hollister' is brain dead? You're just throwing money away on some 'dead' man's estate'!" He raved. I calmly reminded him:

"Look, Stephen, it's still my money, and I have lawyers, accountants, and doctors who could testify I'm still in my right mind. So much so, I could change my will in an hour's time, and it will hold up in any court. So, don't push me, or you may be sorry."

That let the wind out of his sails, and he said he'd be back in an hour. Within that hour I received a call from my family attorney, a good friend, telling me my son had come to him and requested I be declared incompetent. The family attorney had politely told my son to *eat crap and die!* The little turd had not believed me!

I decided not to change my will, but I still had some tricks up my, uh, hospital gown! With some satisfaction I asked my attorney friend to transfer ownership of my secret safety deposit box, which he'd been holding the key for me, to one William Clay Hollister. I told him to be patient, but Mr. Hollister would contact him and would have the proper identification. No one knew what was in the deposit box but me. I had planned to have my attorney make it a surprise inheritance to my oldest son, but not now. Now, if all went well, I could use its contents to augment my new, meager estate. If things went south, then Mr. Hollister would have an estate worth a decent amount.

At visiting hours, only my children showed this time. I'm sure they felt it was anti-climactic, but I put on an Oscar-winning performance as the old man on his deathbed. I acted much frailer than I had the night before, so they could almost hear the death-rattle in my voice. My daughters were all crying, but my sons, I sensed, were silently yelling at me to *get it over with*! I was glad I'd made the decision to *change residences* because I couldn't take their attitudes another night. If I died, then I'd be *someWHERE* else. If the experiment succeeded, I'd be *someONE* else! My last words to my family were:

"I love you kids! Take care of your mother. See you on the other side!" They solemnly filed out.

Now, it was time for the first change in my, hopefully, new life: I went into honest to goodness 'planning mode'! A positive change for me. What should I do? Foremost in my mind was a nagging need to earn a degree, which could be used to advance my success. For this reason, it became an obsessive part of my planning. First, I'd look at what Bill Hollister had going, then make changes as necessary. I wanted to take full advantage of starting over, but it was difficult to fully plan until I knew what I had to work with. A college student he may be, but maybe Bill Hollister was a fool! I doubted it but was anxious to take stock. It's seldom possible for a man to know the moment of his demise, so I was one of the 'lucky' few. I knew, one way or another, Frederick Lloyd Lambson would cease living within a couple hours. Not being religious, I still sent an imploring prayer skyward. It was not totally selfish since I also asked for the Lambson family to be happy and healthy.

Chapter 2

At the conclusion of visiting hours, a hospital usually scales down the staff. The night nurses and doctors hold down the fort until the next day. There's additional staff on call, in case a major event occurs, but for the most part, nurses quietly go about making their rounds and the few doctors, if not actually working on a patient, hang out in the doctor's lounge, hoping they won't be called but ready if they are! A nurse I'd not seen before came into my room and had two attendants transfer me to a gurney, so they could wheel me down to one of the sub-basements.

I know! It sounds corny, to do this procedure in the 'dungeon' of the hospital. My two doctors had their research facilities on that lower floor because it was not used for anything important, as far as the hospital administrator was concerned. When we got to the room where the transfer would take place, I was surprised to see a large amount of expensive looking equipment. I half-expected to see the 'set' from a *Frankenstein* movie. The place looked clean and well-lit. Drs. Sweeney and Randquist were busy at some of the equipment, looking at readings on dials and monitors. I noticed another gurney was already there, occupied with a draped figure.

"Do you mind?" I said to the nurse, nodding my head toward the other gurney.

Looking at the doctors, she received a nod, and I was wheeled alongside my prospective abode. Looking at the adjacent cart, I saw a head growing out from under the sheet. The person was on a respirator, and had electrodes attached all over his head. I couldn't see much of the face, but what I saw was a puffy, florid man who looked like he wouldn't be bad looking if he weren't recovering from a lightning strike! While trying to visualize what he'd look like under normal situations, I saw Dr. Sweeney heading my way.

"Here, Fred! This is what he looked like on his driver's license. Not a bad looking guy, though his coloring is a tad different from yours. His beard is thicker, and he has a full head of hair, still dark. Of course, you aren't bald yet, either! His license says he is six-one and one-ninety, with blue eyes and dark brown hair, though he will probably weigh around one-sixty by now."

"Thanks for the preview, doc! Do you have any confidence in this procedure succeeding?" I implored.

"If I didn't have faith it *could* succeed, I wouldn't have offered it to you. Only time will tell!" he sagely replied.

"How much longer will I be me?" I enquired.

"We're almost ready. We've been down here all afternoon checking the equipment and hooking the probe to Mr. Hollister. We've had much more latitude with him, since he doesn't have visitors, but with you, we can't keep you out of your room too long in case someone checks on you. Whichever way this goes, your present body will expire sometime in the next hour. We'll know almost immediately if your impulses take possession of Mr. Hollister, though he, uh, er, *you* may remain unconscious for hours, or perhaps days, as your psyche takes inventory of your new physical housing. Once you regain consciousness, you may, or may not be in full knowledge of what is happening, but being in unfamiliar territory, you'll most likely not be in control of your motor movements nor your voice. I suspect you'll be able to open your eyes and blink a little, possibly reflexively, and maybe move your fingers a little. Again, only time will tell, as this has all been theory and conjecture up to now," Dr. Sweeney concluded.

"What's the probe like?" I asked.

"It's a bed of needles that will penetrate your brain stem. We can't sedate you because it could affect your brain waves, so we'll give you a local anesthetic because the probe is painful. One of the reasons we need access to your body is so we can try to disguise the puncture wounds on your neck. If an in-depth autopsy were performed, they may question the marks of the probe, but since your present body is expected to pass away at any time, we feel there'll only be a cursory exam, and it may fall to me to perform it. The actual procedure is so complex, I don't think it would do any good to go into the details. It will certainly sound like science fiction. It's still not too late to back out. We don't need your brainwaves to go kicking and screaming into your new home," he said, amusingly.

"What have I got to lose, doc? Let's get on with it. If I don't make it, I want to thank you and Dr. Randquist for your attempts on my behalf. I've directed my accountant to give you two a grant for your research."

"That's very generous of you, Fred, and I assure you we'll do everything we can, even without the grant!"

"I'm sure you will. I didn't tell you about the grant because I wanted special treatment, but to just let you know if it's not successful, I still believe in your work!"

"Thank you, Fred! Okay, let's begin. Here is a little stick in your neck."

I don't really remember much about the rest of it. I closed my eyes, and my brain began going 'round and 'round! I was aware things were happening around me, but I shut it out of my consciousness. I didn't feel the pain of the probe, but I felt the weight on my muscles, as it hung below my neck. I only heard Dr. Sweeney say:

"Good luck, Fred! Here we go!"

How can I describe it? I felt like my mind was racing around in a whirlpool, slowly going down a giant, dark drain hole. Time held no meaning. I felt light and ephemeral. Light, floating; darker and heavier; turbulence, wind-whipped, storm tossed; washed into an eddy, calm, warm, darkness descending like a curtain. Nothing!

Dawning, as I felt cold and lethargic. I tried to open my eyes, but the lids were so heavy. I sensed, rather than heard sounds. I 'felt'? No! I sensed movement against me. I tried to make some sound, but though I felt I was screaming, I heard no sound from me! I struggled to move but could do nothing. I felt exhausted, so I willed myself to cease all exertions. I felt the curtain descend once more. I was in oblivion.

"Garble, garble; patient; monitor looks good; garble, garble; brain activity seems normal," I dimly heard.

I knew that voice but couldn't remember who it was! I tried to open my eyes and they fluttered a little, allowing light to filter through my lashes. I tried harder, batting my lashes frantically.

"Doctor!" someone exclaimed.

"He's regaining consciousness. If you can hear me, Mr. Hollister, close your eyes for a moment, and then bat them again!" A familiar voice.

Relaxing, my eyelids slammed shut, then making an effort, I tried opening them. They fluttered again; then shut; fluttered, shut!

"That's it, Mr. Hollister. I'm so happy you're aware. Just relax, and we'll let you regain more strength." Again, I knew that voice!

But I wanted to scream at the dumb bastard! Why was he calling me Mr. Hollister? My name is... Fred *something*! Fred Lambson. Yeah, that's it! No! Wait! Fred Lambson's supposed to be dead, and he's moved to somewhere else! No! Moved to *someONE* else! Bill something. Yeah! Bill... Hollister! Yeah! William Clay Hollister! I *am* Mr. Hollister. I guess he's not a dumb bastard after all! It was all coming back. I'd survived the transfer! I was euphoric! At least I was aware, in someone else's body. I'd have to see if I could 'function' in someone else's body. I decided to pull the curtain again, to see if I could gain a little more strength.

Feeling buffeted, I felt myself moving and realized I must be on a gurney, headed for... where? I just went with the flow and waited to see what was happening.

"Okay, Mr. Hollister, let's get you down into the whirlpool bath and get some nice massage going for your muscles! Just let me do the work. I got a flotation collar on you, so you won't get your face in the water. That's it, just relax and let the jets do their job."

My attendant was a man, and he was strong, or I was like a child, because he lifted me like one. The water was nice and warm, and the bubbles felt good against my skin. I tried opening my eyes. Blurry images with multiple colors came flooding into my brain. I blinked. The images became sharper, but they seemed different! Did looking through someone else's eyes have to be relearned too? Probably, especially since these were younger eyes than old Fred's. I could see things, and knew pretty much what they were used for, but I couldn't always put a name to them. Every few seconds, a name would click into place, and I knew it was the right one for what I was looking at.

"Well, now I can see you really *do* have blue eyes, like your chart says," my attendant said jovially. "It's good to see you open up them baby blues, Mr. Hollister! I hear you were in the Navy. Me too! I was a corpsman, so I decided to stay in the health care field when I was discharged. Have some good and some bad memories of my time in Uncle Sam's Canoe Club.

How about you? Let me try flexing your legs and get them muscles stretched a little. You been in bed so long, your muscles are losing their tone. You must have done some running. Those leg muscles look like runner's legs to me. Can you move anything today? I've been bringing you here for a week now, and this is the first time I saw any sign of you being alert. You got them burns on your feet and shoulder, but they're about healed. The scabs are looking good, but you'll have scars for a while. Shouldn't tell you about them. Sorry!

"Hey, I'm not moving them hands and arms, and it isn't all the whirlpool! Got to tell the doc about this. It's time to get you out anyhow before you start looking like a prune! Come on, Mr. Hollister. Let's get you out and dried off."

Again, I felt like a feather as this man lifted me out of the bath and dried me with towels before slipping me into a robe and placing me on the gurney once more. I could feel my thumbs and forefingers touching and I exerted myself to squeeze them together. Flexing my muscles, I did a short repetition of squeezing and relaxing. I felt elation, but also fatigue, from this little effort.

That was how my re-incarnation began: First, hearing and understanding the spoken word; Second, opening my eyes and seeing color; Next, having some control over my muscles. It took me two months to walk without assistance. My physical therapist, Roger Napier, was my constant cheerleader as I began moving and eventually walking. We became first name acquaintances.

"Come on, Bill. I know you can last for one lap, at least. Just take your time and rebuild your muscles."

Roger had finally taken me to the track behind the hospital and started me on laps. It took me nearly ten minutes to make the first quarter mile circuit.

"Damn, Roger, I'm done in! I don't know if I can even make it back to my room."

"Sure, you can, Bill. Just think how good that whirlpool is going to feel, then a short walk to your bed. You've got this, Bill," Roger said encouragingly.

By the time I was discharged, I could do the mile in eight minutes. I still had a long way to go, and I found the lightning strike had caused some muscle damage, so I would never be a ballet dancer, but I could do a fair ballroom waltz.

My speech took nearly six months before I felt able to carry on a conversation with anyone besides my speech therapist and doctors. Even Roger had to display great patience with me when I tried to talk to him. Besides the basics of speech, I wanted to have a well-modulated speaking voice, so I took elocution lessons. I remembered I spoke French, Spanish, and Japanese, but the words seemed foreign to my mouth, at first. With constant practice, I eventually felt I had the basic conversational skills in those three languages. I'm not sure what languages the original Bill Hollister knew, but I wanted to make use of the skills I had acquired as Fred Lambson. I'd always enjoyed singing but couldn't carry a tune for beans. Now, I discovered I had a decent baritone singing voice and my speech therapist used this ability to help me learn proper breathing techniques.

During one of the private counseling sessions I had with my two doctors, they revealed some things to me.

"Bill, how do you feel, emotionally? Are you having difficulties reconciling yourself to being 'Bill Hollister,' or are you still identifying as 'Fred Lambson'?" asked Dr. Sweeney.

"I'm getting better at handling it. I still hesitate a second when someone addresses me as Bill Hollister, but I'm improving," I replied.

"Do you think you're ready for this? Dr. Randquist handed me a newspaper clipping.

It was the obituary of Fredrick Lloyd Lambson. It was the one I'd written for myself and left with my son. At least he'd honored my wishes that much! After reading through it, I handed it back.

"It's a bit creepy to read one's own obit!" I replied solemnly.

"We can understand that Bill, but it may give you a little closure. We hope you're not upset by it," Dr. Sweeney said, quietly.

"No. I've reconciled myself to it and have already moved on. I'm just anxious to get out and see what kind of world Bill Hollister has created for himself, and what I can do to change it to my liking," I said, with determination in my voice.

"That's good, Bill. We sincerely hope you get what you want, this time around," said Dr. Randquist.

With all the efforts to rehabilitate me, I was surprised an insurance company would expend so much, but I found out Drs. Sweeney and Randquist were supplementing the insurance by using some of the grant money I had given them. Nearly ten months to the day Fred Lambson died and Bill Hollister was resurrected from a brain-dead hulk, I shook my doctors' hands and gave Roger a hug, then let him push me to the front door of the hospital in a wheelchair, due to hospital policy. I was wearing hospital scrubs since my clothes had been incinerated by the lightning, but I had all the personal effects Bill had come to the hospital with, including nearly forty bucks in the wallet! I took a cab to the address on my driver's license. It was not a bad place, but in need of a good dusting and cleaning. The insurance, with the assistance of the good doctors, had kept my rent paid. The utilities had been temporarily turned off and one of the doctor's staff members had come in and cleaned out the refrigerator and anything perishable from the cupboards.

Everything was foreign to me, but I was determined to make a go of my life as William Clay Hollister. It took a couple weeks to get the lowdown on Bill's life before Mother Nature had given him a 'shot.'

My car had been towed from the university parking lot, and the impound yard magnanimously waived half the storage fees, though I had to pay the towing fee. As could be expected, my vehicle registration had to be renewed and my car insurance re-instated.

In checking on my college record, I also discovered I was struck down on campus, after leaving the library, which accounted for the insurance coverage. The accident had occurred during the end of semester finals, and I had taken all but one final before being sidelined. I was not expected to make up the final, but I had to repeat the course.

I reviewed my transcript and saw Bill Hollister was a history major with a minor in math and had just finished his last semester of his junior year. As part of my continuing rehabilitation, I promised Roger I'd continue to run to remain physically fit. I discovered I enjoyed it and would ruminate while running. To exercise my mind and try to catch up with my new identity, I read through the textbooks I found in the apartment. It made me glad I didn't have to take any sort of validation test to prove I'd earned the college credits listed on my transcript. Always being thirsty for knowledge, and though I didn't earn a degree *per se* as Fred Lambson, I was no dummy. I had a quick mind and I remembered what I read.

Discovering Bill knew several people, but had few friends, I still found myself repeating my story of recovery many times. At least there was no 'significant other' to deal with. My (his) appearance had been altered by the trauma, with a weight loss of between twenty and thirty pounds, so I certainly met expectations for a recovering patient. People around town and on campus who had known 'me' were solicitous, but as is human nature, they didn't want to get too close, as though I were diseased in some way, but it didn't bother me. I also never had anyone from my former (Lambson) family inquire after me, so I decided it would be best to relocate.

Although I was as near normal as anyone could be after being struck by lightning, my doctors were not in favor of me moving too far away.

"Remember, you promised to *give me my head* and not keep me like *a hot-house flower*! I assure you, I'll frequently be in touch with you, and I'm not going clear across country. I just feel I need to get out of my hometown, with a constant fear I'll come face to face with one of my children and be unable to hide my feelings," I argued. Dr. Sweeney seemed sensitive to my feelings and responded:

"All right, Fred, uh, I mean, Bill. We understand. We'd just like to keep a close watch. Make sure you let us know of anything unusual. We'd like you to make an office visit in six months." I reiterated my promise to keep in touch.

Another reason for moving was I didn't want to continue my education at the college in town. When my own children had attended college, I'd sent them to schools with better scholastic reputations, despite the cost. As schools went, the one in town was fully accredited but lacked the prestige of either the Ivy League colleges or the giant bastions of academia such as Columbia or Stanford. Since Bill Hollister was a history major, I thought of how Rice University in Houston was one of the better schools for getting such a degree. California had half dozen different schools with good history degree programs, but I had no desire to be on the West Coast. Then it occurred to me: why was I locked into being a history major?

Realizing I was doing just as I had the first time around: going with the flow; I needed to take a long look at things and decide what I wanted out of my new life, and then see what I had to do to get it! To start, I felt a degree was first priority, but a degree in what? If I were to go on and get a degree in history, what would I be doing the rest of my life? Most likely

I would be teaching, either in secondary schools, or universities. Was that what I wanted to do?

As noble a profession as teaching is, I could not see myself standing before a class of bored students who wondered why they had to take history. After all, they wanted to be either rock stars or rocket scientists, and you didn't need history for those professions, did you? I'd go to the counselor on campus and review my options, given the classes already to my credit.

Making an appointment with a guidance counselor at the college, I arrived and was ushered into her office.

"Mr. Hollister! It's so good to see you after your ordeal. We heard about it when it happened, but we never had updates on your condition, so it's very pleasant to see you've recovered," the counselor gushed. "What brings you in today? How may I help you?" she added, cordially.

"I just wanted to review my transcript and discuss my options based on what I've already accomplished," I supplied.

"Of course. I have your transcript right here. Let me look at it for a second," she said. She hummed as she perused my record. It was a couple minutes before she looked back up and focused on me.

"I see you've completed all your general education courses, which is something most students don't do at first. They just want to get to their major, but in some cases, there are prerequisite courses they must complete, which usually turn out to be general education requirements in the first place. I see you've taken additional courses in both your major and minor, so I can say you're in a good position to complete your degree next year as a senior with both your major and minor intact. You do have an 'incomplete' for a course, due to your, uh, accident. This course would not affect your cumulative number of credits, but you can choose to repeat the course anyway. What would you like to do, Mr. Hollister?" the counselor concluded.

"I'm thinking about transferring to another school due to bad memories," I lied.

"I can see where your accident could elicit those feelings. We'd be sorry to see you go," she lamented.

"Thank you. I was just interested in my options. When I decide, I'll let you know where to send my transcript. Thank you for your time."

"Of course, Mr. Hollister. I'm glad I could accommodate you."

After my appointment with the guidance counselor, I felt much better about my alternatives. I noticed my 'predecessor' had been driven, since I saw few classes like 'Advanced Sandbox' or 'Underwater Basket Weaving,' which is how I often kiddingly referred to 'goof off' classes. Score one for young Mr. Hollister. Given that, I could decide to pursue many different courses of endeavor. His minor was in mathematics, which was more along my line of experience—definitely an option. Though I'd always liked history, I never imagined making a living from it. In my previous field of electronics and aerospace, I was much more into mathematics.

Now! Did I want to parallel my previous life by going back into aerospace? Thinking back to the successful people I'd worked with; I realized their BS/BA degrees were merely the first step. Each earned an MBA, or a Masters in their chosen field, and some went on to their PhDs. So, the actual baccalaureate degree was just the start, if I were after an executive career. Is that what I was after? Would that make me have less regrets? Would it make me feel fulfilled?

Trying to change direction and salvage a career at age twenty-six was not going to be a cakewalk. Not to seem ungrateful, but maybe I shouldn't have demurred about a pubescent body, though in reality, it was never offered. I felt myself attempting to open the proverbial equine maw for closer examination! I told myself I'd better make good this time, or else.

So, I began searching for a not-too-distant school to earn a degree in mathematics. Of course, I knew I could only use the BS degree for a step toward something else. If I were to try for a position of mathematician, I would need a minimum of a Masters, or even a PhD, and I wasn't sure I wanted that. I'd get my BS in math and then most likely go for my Masters. I already knew I'd be competing with grads at least four years younger, so I would just have to be much more brilliant!

Whittling down the list of top schools for mathematics, I finally decided it would either be Northwestern University in Evanston, Illinois, or University of Texas at Austin. These were in the top twenty, but the ones in the top ten were mostly in New England or California. I had no desire to go either place. So... a mental coin toss and Austin, Texas, won! I went online to get the info and enrollment forms. Not wanting to wait too long, I tied up loose ends around town: packed up what belongings I wanted to keep for my own; got rid of the rest; and started on my trek south.

One of the loose ends had been my claiming the safety deposit box. I made an appointment to meet the attorney representing Fredrick Lambson. Upon entering his office, I didn't notice how I acted at home there, and he gave me an odd look. I presented my credentials and said I'd been told about the bequest from Mr. Lambson and was there to claim it. Asking how I knew Mr. Lambson, I explained—that is, lied about—how I had met him briefly, just before I was struck down by lightning. After I recovered, I discovered he'd left me cash in my savings account and a rumor of a further bequest, waiting to be claimed. Explaining why it took so long to contact him, the attorney seemed satisfied, but he threw in a quick quiz to see if I'd really met Mr. Lambson. I had to really suppress a giggle and had a strong compulsion to admit everything. The only thing keeping me from it was credibility!

Asking me if I knew what was in the box, I told him I didn't have the vaguest idea. He admitted he didn't either. It was like a treasure hunt. For all we knew, it could have been an old pair of shoes! Of course, I knew better, but I played along. I told him I was already ten-thousand dollars richer, due to Mr. Lambson's gift to my savings account. Anything else would be an additional windfall. I knew he wanted to come with me to the bank, just to see what was in the box, but his professionalism would not allow him to suggest it. After receiving the key and identity papers, I thanked him and went directly to the bank.

Not to put too fine a point on it: I already knew what I would find in the box. Let me say it was a combination of negotiable assets anyone could have received and converted to cash very easily. There were bearer bonds and gold coins, which would cash out to around one hundred thousand dollars. I had amassed this little pot as a 'rainy day fund,' just in case. It was a nice beginning to my new life and would augment my working capital. I knew I couldn't live off this new money for long, so planned to get my veterans benefits flowing again from my G.I. educational fund. I needed the benefits, and I (Fred) had lost a good portion of my Viet Nam Era benefits because Congress ended them in 1989, before I had a chance to use them all. I wasn't going to throw them away this time! I splurged on one thing before leaving town. I wasn't too sure about my used car, so I went to a 'previously owned' car lot and bought a two-year-old Subaru Outback station wagon. As Fred, I had known the salesman and I knew how he operated, so I worked him for the most reliable car rather than the best financial deal. If I was frugal, I could delay finding a job for a while.

Chapter 3

Arriving in Austin, Texas, on a Sunday, things were pretty quiet. Back in 1980, I had been in the city once before, but only for a couple days. Of course, in the intervening thirty-odd years, the city had changed immensely. Before I moved, I'd researched the layout of the city using Google Maps and now had the basic lay of the land.

I was too old to want to live on campus, so I picked up a Sunday paper and began looking for a place to live. I found a small home, a couple miles from the campus. Housing is always a problem near a college, or university. In short supply, landlords usually demanded premium rents. Being older and more astute, business-wise, I struck a deal I could live with. Because the place was furnished, I moved right in. In the *old days*, Blue Laws would have prevented me from buying some items on a Sunday, but now it was just alcohol and car dealers affected on Sunday. So, I went to the store to buy the necessities for setting up a household. Unpacking and storing these things took the remainder of the day, but not too late to get in a mile run.

Monday mid-morning found me driving over to the campus. I knew the school was within two weeks of the end of a semester. I planned to be here now, on purpose. I could familiarize myself with the campus, check on my application process, and possibly pick up credit for a couple classes by 'challenging' the course, also called 'credit by exam.' Not all universities allowed this, and it was an 'iffy' thing because professors like to think you don't know anything about their subject unless you take their course. I won't go into my rant here, but in some cases the professor wrote the textbook he's teaching from, and the student is required to purchase it! The course ends up being subjective from the professor's viewpoint. Therefore, there are usually problems transferring credits from one school to another, especially if they're in different states.

This is why I had Bill's old school send his transcript to the University of Texas at Austin, or UTA, so they could evaluate the courses to see what they would accept in transfer. When I arrived at the school and inquired about the outcome of the analysis, I was told they'd accept all of my lower-level courses, and some of my upper-level ones. There was one class each in history, economics, and mathematics that would not transfer. It would be up to the Dean, the respective department head, and the course professor as to whether I could try for credit without taking the course. It was worth it if I could get out of taking a couple courses. I was on a tight schedule for completion of my degree, so I submitted my request to challenge the three courses.

On my way out of the Admin building, I scanned the two or three bulletin boards I saw. Bulletin boards are a great way to see what was happening on either a military base or a college campus. A lot of things were for sale, and there were services offered (babysitting for married students with children, etc.). There were ads for a number of student groups (e.g., Young Democrats, Young Republicans, LGBTQ support, Chess Club, etc.). One of them caught my eye: it was a poster for a Firearms Club. After all, this *was* Texas!

I'd always owned firearms as an adult and knew how to use them. I didn't hunt but shot targets, trap and skeet. I had my concealed-carry permit; I should say—*when I was Fred Lambson, I had one.* Very few of the other clubs interested me since I was not here for the social aspect of college life. I just thought a firearms club would give me an outlet for the inherent stress. They met at the firing range just off campus, and they had regular competitions. It would be a good way to let off some steam, firing at targets. A contact name, 'I. Grey,' and phone number were at the bottom, so I wrote them down. Maybe they could give me some recommendations on where to purchase a pistol. I hadn't thought about it before now, but I wondered what happened with my—that is, Fred's—gun collection? My family had their own guns, so they probably sold mine! I also made a mental note to check on a course to get a concealed carry permit for my new identity!

"You interested in the gun club?" a voice behind me asked.

Turning around, I saw a short, stocky guy I estimated at twenty years old. His eyes had a twinkle in them, revealing he'd be a friendly sort, and I should get to know him, so I said:

"I was thinking of it! I just got into town and won't start until next semester, but I was getting my registration straightened out. I left all my firearms behind, so I'll have to find another one if I decide to join. My name is Bill Hollister!"

"Hi! I'm Tim Latham. I'm a sophomore. I just came up from Kingsville before last semester. I was going to Texas A&M."

"Yeah, I heard it used to be called Texas A&I!"

"That was a long time ago!"

"Yeah, I guess it was," I replied.

I had to be more careful! Being stationed in Kingsville when I was in the military, in the late seventies/early eighties, I automatically dropped back into my old persona, but a lot had changed since then, and I didn't need anyone quizzing me about how I knew so much about 'ancient' history!

"What class are you in?" Tim queried.

"Well, I should be starting my senior year, but had to drop out for almost a year, due to illness. Now it all depends on whether all my credits from my last school will transfer. I was just applying for permission to challenge a couple courses."

"*Good luck*! I heard a lot of guys try but very few actually get away with it! What's your major?" Tim exclaimed.

"Math! What's yours?" I answered.

"Same, but my minor's in computer science, and I'll probably get a job doing that before I make use of my math degree!"

"You're going to stop after your BS?" I asked.

"Yeah, why?"

"I just thought you'd go on and get your Masters!"

"I gotta get a job first, to pay for my student loans," Tim opined.

"Oh. I get you."

"Yeah, I'm up to my ears in student loans."

"I'm not, yet! I got my G.I. Bill," I bragged.

"Cool! I thought you looked a bit older than the rest!"

"Yeah. Say, where's a good place to buy a pistol for the club?"

"You'd better talk to Izzy about that," Tim responded.

"Izzy?"

"Isabel Grey. She doesn't like anyone calling her Izzy to her face, so I shouldn't, but she's the president of the Firearms Club and the best shooter on the team! If you want to know about things like the club and where to go for shooting supplies, she's the one to ask."

"A woman is the president of the gun club? I saw the 'I. Grey' and assumed it was Israel or Ishmael or Ichabod!" I exclaimed.

"Nope. It's Isabel. I think she likes to be president so it'll intimidate the guys. I wouldn't want to get in her way," Tim said, warningly.

"So, where do I find Ms. Grey?" I queried.

"Mizz? You okay? Just call her Isabel! If you call her 'Mizz

Grey,' she'll be pissed!"

"Just trying to be polite!" I remarked.

"We're kind of informal around here, except for the Izzy thing," Tim added.

"Gotcha! But where does *Isabel* hang, when she's not in class or off campus?"

"She's usually along the West Mall or at her dorm... Blanton Dormitory. She has a posse of sorts, and they usually gather in the main cafeteria at lunch and on the West Mall in the afternoon," Tim said informatively.

"She has a posse?" I asked incredulously.

"Well, where I come from, that's what they call a small gang! Around here, we call her group The Gaggle!" Tim explained.

"The Gaggle? A posse?" I acted confused.

"I don't think they know every guy on campus calls them The Gaggle, but it's the elite group of babes on campus," Tim said admiringly.

"So... Isabel is a babe?" I said, awestruck.

"Oh, yeah! The Queen Babe, but she's untouchable, especially with the *gun thing*," Tim warned.

"Why? Does she hate men?" I inquired.

"Don't think so, but no guy gets very far before he loses interest. Of course, *I've* never made a run on her! She'd change her mind. *Not!* She's real nice at the gun club, so I don't know where she got her reputation," Tim told me wonderingly.

"And you were just going to let me walk right into her and make a fool of myself?" I said accusingly.

"Well, I figured if you wanted to know about her, you'd ask, and you did! Score one for you, Bill!" Tim retorted.

"How do you shoot?" I said inquisitively.

"I hold my own. I'm not in Izzy's class, but I do okay," he answered humbly.

"Good for you! I haven't shot competitively for years, but

I think it'd be a good stress reliever."

"Yeah! Well. I've got a class in... five minutes... across campus!" Tim said dismissively.

"Sorry to make you late," I apologized.

"The professor's never there on time. I got at least fifteen minutes, so it's no sweat! See you around, Bill," Tim tossed off as he turned to go.

"Yeah, hope to, Tim. Take care!"

Well, it was after lunch, so I'd have to look her up this afternoon. I had a map of the campus, so I shouldn't have trouble finding the West Mall, but spotting Isabel Grey could be a challenge. I didn't want to go off campus and then back on, so I decided to check out the student bookstore. Luckily, it wasn't far from the Admin building. I looked at the textbooks on the classes I was going to challenge, hoping to find something familiar. No luck! In fact, I wasn't sure which professors I'd be sent to, if the challenges were approved. I decided it would be appropriate to get a supply of notebooks, folders, and sweatshirts emblazoned with the school logo and mascot: Bevo, the Texas Longhorn! I felt foolish, until I told myself I was a twenty-six-year-old and had to fit in. I put my purchases in my car and headed in the direction of the West Mall. I was in no real hurry to find the woman, since I had time before the next semester, but at the moment, I had nothing else to do but sit at home.

The Malls on campus were like the Mall in Washington, D.C., in that they were long strips of land, or lawn. This one extended at least half a mile, situated between buildings, and being intersected by a street every block. Walking along the Mall, I saw several student groups. One such group was exclusively girls, and they were all attractive, so I assumed I may have found The Gaggle. Slowly approaching the group, I knew they were aware of me, as a few turned to watch me come up to them.

"Excuse me, but is there an Isabel Grey in this group?" I queried.

One woman, whose back had been toward me turned only her head and answered: "I'm Isabel Grey. What do you need?"

Tim had been correct: she was the best looking of them all. Her dark brown hair was cut just at her neckline and was slightly curly. She had piercing green eyes which seemed on the verge of sparkling. An aquiline nose dropped gracefully to end above a sculpted pair of lips colored a subdued deep red. I had paused a moment to drink in her beauty, and she must have thought I didn't hear her!

She repeated: "I said I was Isabel. What do you want?"

"Oh, uh, Tim Latham said I should speak to you about joining the Firearms Club," I fumbled.

"The semester's almost over," Isabel retorted.

"I know, but I thought I could get a jump on next semester!" I replied back, matching her tone.

"Are you interested in just plinking at targets, or are you interested in competition?" she questioned.

"I'm a bit rusty, but I want to compete. Tim told me you could steer me toward a good place to purchase a firearm. I left all mine up north, as I didn't think I'd have any opportunity here," I said informatively.

"Excuse me, girls. I need to talk to Mr. ...?"

"William Clay Hollister. Uh, Bill Hollister," I supplied.

"Well, William Clay Hollister... may I call you Clay?" she asked coquettishly.

"If you'd like! I answer better to Bill, but it's fine if you prefer Clay!" I said accommodatingly.

"You seem amenable. What do you shoot, Clay?" Isabel enquired.

"I've shot nearly everything, but I prefer 9mm or .40 cal. I competed with .45 cal., 9mm, and .22 target rifles," I supplied.

"I'd like to see you shoot! Could you meet me at the firing

range tonight? Oh, I'm not sure I can make it. Can you text me at seven?" Isabel asked.

"I'm a bit old-fashioned, so could I call you? I'm not great at texting. And, yes, I can meet you. I passed the range on my way to the campus," I apologized.

"You live off campus then?" she questioned.

"Yes, I rented a small house not far from here," I replied.

"Are you and your family settled yet?" she asked.

"No family and it's a furnished house, so not much to settle," I responded.

"Oh, okay then, give me a call at this number at seven sharp!" she said dismissively. Handing me a card, she turned and went back to her posse. Glancing at the card, I noted: no title, just name and number, embossed. Unassuming. Not real stuck on herself! Very attractive! I tucked the card in my shirt pocket and looked at the group of girls once more. They were already in full cry as a gaggle, and quick glances my way let me know I may've been a topic of conversation. It was the first time in my new self I was excited about interaction with a woman! I guess some of my lesser nerve endings were beginning to be activated! But I berated myself for being so easily sidetracked.

A note on the bulletin board about tonight being Mongolian BBQ at one of the eateries on campus had caught my eye earlier. I loved Mongolian BBQ as Fred but didn't know how Bill would react. I decided to drive to the house, clean up, and then return to campus for dinner. By then, it would be about time to call Isabel.

Parking a good walk away from the restaurant, so I could help settle my meal on my return, it was after a pretty good dinner I sauntered in the general direction of the car. Keeping an eye on the time, I was almost to my car when a woman ran into me. I caught her to prevent her from falling. Holding her in my arms, I looked into the green eyes of Isabel Grey! The startled look in her eyes changed to amusement as she recognized me.

"Well, I bet you ate Mongolian BBQ tonight!" she said, smiling.

"I'm sorry! I hope it's not too offensive," I lamented. I let her go and stepped back. She let out a little tinkling laugh.

"No, of course not! I love that stuff! I've just never been this close to someone else eating it. I'm sorry I wasn't watching where I was going. I was rushing back to my dorm, so I'd be there when you called. I left my cell phone there on the charger."

"I can still call you if you want to rush back to your dorm," I said, smiling.

"You just want to watch me running away, so you can ogle me!" she chided.

"I never thought of that, but it sounds like a good idea. Better hurry!" My smile was so wide my mouth hurt.

"Oh, you!" She slapped lightly at my arm.

I grabbed her upper arms loosely and looked into her eyes once more. For the life of me, I don't know why I did it, but I felt a sudden compulsion come over me. I leaned in and kissed her on the mouth. It surprised her so much, her mouth was partially open, and I had to really fight the impulse to stick my tongue into her mouth. I immediately backed off!

"I'm so sorry, Isabel! That was totally wrong of me! I've never done that before! Please forgive me?" I was penitent.

Eyes still wide as dinner plates and mouth still open in surprise, her eyes finally narrowed, and she looked at me oddly.

"You, Mr. William Clay Hollister, will bear watching! Now, are you still going to call me?"

"Yes! In about..."—I glanced at my watch—"seven and a half minutes," I chortled.

"I've got to change clothes, so call me, and I'll tell you when to meet me at the range! Now, you walk away, and I'll walk away, and no one is to watch the other! Deal?"

"Deal!" I vowed.

Chapter 4

When I called at seven p.m. on the dot, she picked up after the first ring.

"Yes! Is this the forward guy I just encountered on the Mall?" she accused.

"Hello, Isabel. Yes, it's me. Again, I apologize," I confessed. Her laugh through the phone was just as enjoyable as it had been face to face.

"It's okay! I'm just going to have to keep my distance, or we could be in trouble. Meet me at the range between seven-forty-five and eight. I'll bring a couple of my pistols, and I'll check you out on them. The range is open 'til ten, so we have time to shoot a couple boxes of ammo, which I usually just buy there. Is that all right?" she asked.

"Sure. I'll be there!" I promised.

"Great! Bye!" she said succinctly.

No dawdling on the phone for Ms. Grey. She hung up, and I was left holding the phone to my ear. I'd called her from my cell phone, sitting in my car on campus. I guess she needed extra time to change, so I just drove off campus, and it took me five minutes to get to the range. Parking in the lot, I debated whether to go inside or wait in the car. I opted for the car so I could see her drive in and meet her outside.

I was really surprised to see her peddling a bike into the lot, which explained why she needed the extra time. Getting out of my car, I met her at the bike rack near the entrance. Removing a backpack from the handlebars, she put it over her shoulder. Being from the old school, I took it from her, which got me a speculative look. The bag was heavy, as I would expect if she brought the promised pistols.

"I called ahead for a lane, and they told me it wasn't busy. I brought a 9 and a 40 to see how you do with each. Let's get two boxes of each, and then I can shoot the gun you're not using," she advised.

Walking up to the counter, the range guy greeted Isabel by name, and she introduced me. She asked for the ammunition, and when she reached for her wallet, I told her it was on me. I also paid for use of two adjacent lanes and a half-dozen paper targets. Because I was with a member, I got the discount! She was looking at me again.

"Either you're trying to impress me, or you're a throwback to the dark ages! That's not meant as a slam. Just an observation," she complimented.

"You've taken time out of your—no doubt—busy schedule to show me the range and evaluate me for possible membership in your club. I realize it may be anachronistic, but I was raised to be a gentleman, my behavior on the Mall a little while ago notwithstanding. It's the least I can do!" I assured her.

"Thank you, Bill," she said brightly

"You're welcome, Isabel."

Knowing her way around the range, she led me to the lanes we'd rented. Getting the backpack from me, she opened it. Inside were two padded and zippered pistol packs. She also had two sets of ear protectors and safety glasses. I adjusted the ear protectors she handed me to my head and put on the glasses.

"What do you want to shoot first?" she asked.

"Whichever. You choose," I replied.

She handed me one of the cases, and it turned out to be a .40 caliber Smith & Wesson, M&P. I (Fred) had one just like it. I showed familiarity with the weapon and had the magazine loaded in short order. She'd been watching and seemed satisfied I was not gaming her. The targets were mounted and run out to twenty-five yards.

"Okay, just get the feel of the gun for the first magazine, then on the second we'll use another target and try for some grouping," Isabel directed.

"Right!" I agreed.

I calmly fired Isabel's pistol, finding it felt familiar, but slightly different in my hands. My hand-to-eye coordination had not been tested to this extent before now. I managed to see where it was hitting and made some slight eye-to-sight adjustments. Twelve shots are not a lot when you're trying hard to impress someone.

"Do you need another magazine to get used to my pistol?" she asked.

"Yes, please," I pleaded.

"Go ahead!" she allowed.

I felt much better after the second twelve. If I'd been doing this on my own, I would have shot a hundred rounds through a strange gun before trying for grouping, but I wasn't going to complain about it. Isabel had just been plinking, warming up on her 9mm. We ran the targets back up and took cursory glances at each. I was a bit ashamed of mine, when I looked at hers, but I didn't say anything. Changing targets, we ran them back out and loaded up for another round. After emptying the magazine, Isabel asked me to move my grouping down and try some rapid fire with the next load. I complied, and then she brought the targets in. She looked critically at my target, and I looked at hers. She was *good*! For not shooting before with my new self, I didn't do too badly either, if I should say so.

"Well, with a strange weapon, you did better than most club members do with their personal pieces! I'd like you in the club. We have a competition this Saturday, but we have a full roster, so you won't be needed. That will give you time to get your own handgun or two and practice. Let's see how you do with the 9!" she directed.

Before we were finished, we'd bought four more boxes of ammo, but Isabel insisted on paying for them. We had a good time, and I learned a little more about her, and she learned more about me! I hated it when I got a quick look of pity after I told her about my lightning strike. Luckily, it didn't last, and she said:

"It looks like you've no lasting damage. You seem perfectly normal!" she commented.

I put on a broad smile and a sly look in my eye.

"I think one of the side effects is a compulsive urge to grab certain women and kiss them!" I got that wonderful tinkling laugh in return.

"I suppose I'll have to make allowances, then, but try to keep it under control—or at least warn a girl!"

We cleaned up our area and re-stowed her backpack. She gave me the names of a few places to buy guns in the area. She also gave me the name of an instructor for a concealed carry permit. Wanting to tell her I had one in my last state, I had to remind myself it was in Fred's name, and I didn't have access to it anyway! Since it was nearly ten at night, I asked her if I could put her bike on my roof rack and give her a ride back to the dorm. Pausing for a few seconds to consider the offer, she finally agreed, thanking me for the offer. Driving under the speed limit, I tried to make the trip back on campus last as long as possible. I parked in front of Blanton Dorm, she didn't rush to get, out and we spent nearly twenty minutes just talking about whatever came up.

"So, what got you interested in shooting?" I asked her.

"My dad was an avid shooter, and since I was an only child, he used to take me to the range. I realized I liked it and was pretty good."

"Tim Latham thinks you do it to intimidate guys." She

laughed at the remark.

"I don't, but it gives me a built-in safety net, so usually no one messes with me."

"The way you shoot, I'm not surprised," I said, smiling.

Finally, she said she should be getting to bed so she could attend an early class.

Getting out and taking her bicycle down from the roof, I put the kickstand down and put her backpack on the handle-bars. This left us facing each other.

"Isabel, you should run because my compulsive behavior is beginning to surface again." She smiled. "Let me help you with that!"

Coming into my arms, she tilted her head up so I could lean into her lips. As my mouth descended on hers, she opened her lips slightly and I found her tongue slipping inside of me. Her arms tightened around my neck, and she lifted her body up so our faces were on the same level. Extending to nearly half a minute, she seemed reluctant to pull back but finally did so. As she relaxed her arms around my neck, she slid back to her side of the bike, keeping her eyes locked on mine. She smiled.

"Now, I think I better run! Thanks for the ride, and for the fun at the range. You have my number, and I'll get you up to speed on texting. I'll be in the main cafeteria at noon if you want to stop by. See you!" she commented.

"Night, Isabel. See you!" I sighed.

While driving back to my house, I told myself the evening had gone pretty well. I had kissed Isabel twice, and she wasn't peeved at me! Tomorrow, I would see about buying a couple pistols and some accessories. If I could, I would be at the cafeteria at noon. Feeling very strange about what was happening I tried to remember having this sort of thing happen as a young man in Fred's body. I couldn't! Maybe it was because he didn't go to college! I again cautioned myself to not be distracted from my main goals here at UTA. I could not fail this time around.

Chapter 5

The next morning, I slept in, figuring the gun shops wouldn't be open until nine or so. As I was lazing around the house, my cell phone rang. It was the university. My request for 'credit by exam' had already gone up the chain, and I had conferences with professors from the classes I had requested. The first, with the history professor, was that morning. The other two were for Wednesday. I hurried, got ready, and made it to the appointment with time to spare, but I had no idea what would be required of me. Most likely the professor would see I had never been to a college in my life! As it turned out, I was glad I'd read all those textbooks of Bill's back home. It had been good therapy, and I'd either refreshed my memory of things, or I had learned new things.

Professor Jeffrey Taggert, reportedly, was a piece of work! He thought history was the only subject worth knowing, and felt he knew more than most. Being only forty-five, he was also a Liberal. As much as I liked history, he made me grateful I had changed majors. I wouldn't want to be like him. Of course, I didn't show any of these opinions. Sitting in front of his desk, I waited for him to speak. He had been reading a copy of my transcript.

"I see you've taken quite a few history classes. Are you going to major in history?"

"No, sir. I thought I would, but decided I should make that my minor, and go for math as my major. The chances for employment are better," I replied.

"Probably a wise choice. For history professors, it's a labor of love, and we don't mind not making all the money in the world!"

"Uh, yes, sir!"

"So, what happened in May of 1886 in Chicago? Please don't say the Great Chicago Fire," the professor curtly exclaimed.

"Yes, sir. The Great Chicago Fire was in 1871! The Haymarket Riot took place in Chicago on May 4th, 1886. It was essentially a labor dispute between the fledgling labor unions and industry. They were reportedly working to establish the eight-hour workday as the standard. There is still controversy about who started the riot. A few anarchists were arrested, and four were tried and executed. There were simultaneous demonstrations in New York, Detroit, and other major cities, but none gained the notoriety of the Haymarket Affair."

"I'm impressed! That's a relatively obscure event, and you seemed to be well founded, knowledge-wise. We may disagree, philosophically!"

"Yes, sir!"

"Quite good, young man! I understand you feel ill-used, since you've taken a history class which will not transfer. So, I invite you to take my semester final exam with the rest of my classes on Wednesday. I will award you the grade you earn on the exam."

"Thank you very much, sir! What textbook will you base it on, so I can study up?" I exclaimed. Giving me the name of the textbook, he congratulated me on my initiative. I needed to let his secretary know by Friday if I intended to take the final. I shook his hand, and he ushered me out of his office. I guess he wasn't so bad, after all! It was now eleven-forty-five.

Walking into the main cafeteria at a little after noon, I spotted The Gaggle right away. They were holding court at one of the central tables. The core of the group seemed to number five, with a retinue of probably five more, and they all exuded an air of superiority. Isabel was conspicuous in the middle of the group. I picked up a tray and went through the serving line, paying for my salad and drink at the cashier kiosk. Walking past the group, I made eye contact with Isabel but kept walking to a table twenty feet away. Sitting down, I began eating lunch. As I watched her, Isabel said something to her minions and got up from the table. She didn't just walk my way: I would have to say she... sashayed! Noticing eyes all around the dining room being drawn to her, I couldn't help but feel good because she had let me kiss her. No doubt she had many admirers, and I had to admit I was one of them. When she reached my table, she sat opposite me and looked down at my tray. Looking back up, she said:

"Hi, Billy Clay! How're you doing today?"

"Another name? Can't make up your mind what to call me? Don't worry! I'd come to most anything you called, as long as I knew you meant me!" I grinned at her.

"Such a flirt! My gosh!" She was smiling too.

"I'm fine. Did we talk about me challenging some courses?" I asked.

"Yes, but you'd just turned in the application," she replied.

"I know, but they must have little to do because I was called this morning and had my first interview at ten!" I bragged.

"Really? What prof did you meet with?"

"Professor Taggert, for history." I answered.

"Yeah, Ugh! I know him. I have a final with him next week."

"On Wednesday?" I asked.

"Yes. How did you know?"

"I was invited to take it also."

"Oh, neat!" she replied, "I can't believe he'd do that, without taking the class?"

"Well, it's better than taking it next semester. I need to quit looking gift horses in the mouth. Maybe we can study together!"

"What are you talking about... gift horses' mouths... what does that mean?"

"Sorry. I grew up around a lot of older people, and I picked up some old sayings most people don't hear these days. To make it short: I shouldn't turn down the chance to take the final, so I don't have to take history again. Get it?" I murmured.

"Oh! Okay! Sure, we can try studying together, but I warn you: I don't mess around when I study! I'm all business. My friends don't invite me to study sessions anymore, because they party, and get only a little studying done," Isabel chirped.

"I'm with you! Studying is a serious thing," I said solemnly.

"Okay! We agree?" she avowed.

"Yup!" I agreed.

"Fine. Now! Do you want to really shake things up, and be the talk of the campus?" She questioned.

"I'm not going to strip down to my BVDs and walk across campus!" I said, smiling.

I got the tinkling laugh.

"No, stupid! I'm pretty much considered a man-hater, though it's not true. I don't know why guys shy away from me," she wondered.

"Oh, come on! You're drop-dead gorgeous, and it probably intimidates them!" I scoffed.

"I don't seem to intimidate you," she remarked.

"Well, it was the gun club. I felt at ease asking about that. I think they're afraid to ask you out."

"No. I've been asked out, but they usually only ask once, and then they're on to other women! I don't think I act like a bitch, but I'm not easy, either!"

"No, you're pleasant, and fun to be around, and I'm glad I got to know you first! If I had just run into you in a class, I would probably be intimidated, a bit, too. Your beauty makes you seem untouchable! And your retinue is imposing, too!"

"Well, thank you! I'd never heard the guy's side of it! What I was getting at, though, was something to stir things up around here. I thought if you were to kiss me, here, in front of all these people, we'd be the talk of campus before the afternoon was over!" she advanced.

"The idea is certainly tempting, but they'd probably say you were being charitable by being kind to the new guy!" I joked.

Oh, man! Did I see storm clouds forming? Before I could try and ameliorate the situation, she cut me off. "Don't say that! You're a nice guy, and you're good looking, and I like you!" she admonished.

"I'm sorry, Iz! I was trying to be funny, but I guess I wasn't. Thanks for the compliments, and I like you too! And I apologize for calling you 'Iz'! I know you don't like it," I pleaded.

"Well, okay, but don't put yourself down again. As far as my name is concerned: I don't mind if *certain* people call me Iz or Izzy, but I don't want everyone doing it. You're allowed, but only between us, all right?" Isabel whispered.

"You bet! Thank you for granting me the privilege."

"Bill, I don't understand you. You look and act like a 'macho type' guy, but you're so polite, and sensitive!" she queried.

"Just the way I am! I like people and like to treat them well, hoping they'll reciprocate," I supplied.

"I like it! So, what do you think about my idea?" she asked.

"You mean for causing a scandal?" I questioned.

She giggled so cutely, I found myself wanting to grab her and hug her.

"Yeah!" She giggled again.

"Well, I don't know why it's only in your presence, but I do feel a compulsion coming over me," I confessed and got that tinkly laugh again.

We both stood and I walked around to her side of the table. Not all eyes were on us, but there were enough we figured to go for it. Placing my hands on her upper arms, I pulled her toward me and gently pressed my lips against hers. She had puckered up but relaxed her lips, so it was nice and cushiony. We did not spar with our tongues, but people knew we were really kissing. I noticed even The Gaggle was in awe! We then backed away, looking at each other.

"So, what're you doing this afternoon?" Isabel queried.

"I need to go find a pistol or two!" I answered.

"Okay, good luck. Will you call me about four-thirty?" she asked.

"Sure. I'll try texting, but if I foul up, I'll call," I confessed.

"Okay. Bye, now!"

She flounced off toward her posse. They were waiting for her, to get an explanation for her inexcusable behavior. This left me to finish eating, though I wasn't very hungry for food!

Knowing we weren't acting our age; we were still having fun. This was college, and the average age for a student was about twenty-one. Izzy had told me she was twenty-four. She'd worked for a couple years before college to help her parents with tuition. I told her about my military, so we were both above average in age, but it just didn't matter. This time around, I was determined to be serious about my studies to earn my degree, but right now I could have a little fun. I didn't want to be seventy again and regret not having *some* fun.

Chapter 6

Finding a firearm was easy, but finding one I really liked was not! During the afternoon, I visited three sporting goods stores. Between the three, I saw just about every make and model of firearm on the market. I preferred either Smith & Wesson, Ruger, or Beretta, but there were newer makes and models out. Two out of the three stores had their own range, so I had a chance to rent a pistol to try it out. I ended up buying three different pistols: a 9mm, a .40 cal., and a .45 cal. I was not a .45 nut, but thought it may be handy in case there was competition in that caliber. Since Texas didn't have a waiting period for buying handguns, I just had to wait for them to do a background check. It took a little longer, since I hadn't been in Texas very long, but—as I already knew—Bill Hollister had a clean record. I was now set to participate in club activities.

By the time I'd shopped for, and purchased my guns, it was getting on to four-thirty, so I took my goodies home. I'd also picked up some accessories, such as speed loaders, a cleaning kit, and a gun safe. I put everything in my spare bedroom and pulled out my phone. I fumbled my way through a text, then said 'to hell with it' and called. The other end answered on the second ring.

"Hello, is this the compulsive kisser? I just got your text too."

"Hi, Izzy! I called just in case my text didn't work! How was your afternoon? Did your friends rake you over the coals for letting me kiss you in public?" I asked and got her cute giggle!

"Ooooh, they really razzed me about that! They couldn't believe 'Little Ms. Deepfreeze' would let a guy she just met kiss her in front of everyone! Most of them were around when you and I met yesterday. They don't understand the attraction," she replied.

"I know how they feel..." I muttered.

"Don't go there, buster!" she snapped.

"Yes ma'am!" I said penitently.

"No, seriously! I just feel at ease with you. You're different from other guys I've met!"

"Yeah, I'm special!" I chuckled.

"Don't push it!" she laughed.

"Yes, ma'am!" I repeated.

"That's better! Now, what about you? Did you find a firearm this afternoon?" she queried.

"Yep! I got three of them!" I bragged.

"Three? How can you afford that? Oh, sorry! I'm being rude and nosey," she back peddled.

"That's okay! I've a little money put away," I returned.

"Well, I shouldn't pry. So, when're you going to try them?" she quizzed.

"I was thinking about going back to the range tonight. You wanna go?" I asked.

"I can't. I have plans," she admitted.

"All right. Maybe next time," I said hopefully.

"Aren't you curious about what I'm doing?" she vented.

"None of my business! Besides, it was probably planned before I even met you! Izzy, as much fun as it is to be with you, I've no claim on your time. You're a very popular woman and involved in a lot of things. I doubt you spend many evenings staying in your room," I obliged.

"Bill, you're so strange! Most guys think they own a girl after a couple kisses!" Isabel lamented.

"I'm not *most guys*," I said humbly.

"I'm beginning to realize it! Anyway, I have to go into town with the girls. We'll be out until at least eight! Are you going to be at the range that late?" Isabel said.

"I could be if there was a reason. Why?" I asked.

"We're taking Cyndee's car, and I could have them drop me at the range. Could you bring me home after?" Isabel replied.

"After what?" I asked.

"Whatever. We could just spend a little time together if you want."

"It would be great being with you, and it would be no problem to take you home."

"Cool! See you at the range around *eight-ish*," Isabel remarked.

"Sounds good," I agreed.

"'Kay. Bye!" Isabel said breathily.

"Bye."

After ending the call, I sat feeling like I was sixteen, again. I had to take stock: after meeting Isabel yesterday, I'd seen her four times in twenty-four hours, a couple times for less than ten minutes; three out of those four times, I'd kissed her! Events were going way too fast! Knowing we were both mid-twenty adults, I felt obliged to slow things down. We were both here for a degree, and we didn't need distractions. As much as I wanted to call her back and cancel tonight's meeting, I figured it'd be just the time to talk things over. I didn't want to hurt her and was sure this was just a quick flirtation on her part. She'd been in college for four years and knew the ropes. Despite my supposed experience, this was a new environment for me. And, I hadn't even attended my first class session!

The guy behind the counter at the range remembered me from the night before. I bought a range membership, which gave me five free visits a month and a discount on additional uses of the range. I also got a discount on anything I bought there. It was worth the cost. Again, the range wasn't crowded, and I got a lane away from others. Putting two boxes of ammo through each of my three pistols, I was happy with how they felt and shot. Finishing up about seven-forty-five, I spent time talking with the counterman until Isabel arrived around eight-fifteen. When she walked in, I just grabbed my gear and headed for the door. I could see the counterman was disappointed: Isabel was indeed eye candy!

When we were in my car, I asked where we were going.

"Let's go to your place, and I'll help you clean your pistols!" she supplied.

"You're not really dressed for that! You'll get your pretty blouse oily," I cautioned.

"I can clean guns in my Prom formal!" she bragged.

"Oh, excuse me! I'm just a slob guy, who gets everything all over!" We laughed.

"Are you sure that's what you want to do? I can clean them after I take you home," I suggested.

"Yes. I'm sure. It gives me an excuse to see your place," she remarked.

"You don't need an excuse. Just ask. Besides, we could always clean the guns on my car hood outside your dorm!" I joked.

"Not me, buster!" she said smugly.

"Okay, my place it is!"

Pulling into my driveway, I got out and went around to open her door, which was already half-open. She looked at me oddly but said nothing. Grabbing my bag out of the back seat, I showed her inside. While she looked around, I found a newspaper and spread it on the kitchen table. Unloading the three weapons onto the table, I went into the spare bedroom and got my cleaning gear. I also got an old shirt from my closet and handed it to her.

"Just in case," I said.

"Thank you! Bill, are you sure you're only twenty-six? You seem so chivalrous, like you're not from this century," she mused.

"Along with learning all those old sayings, I was taught to be a gentleman from the 'old school.' I was taught to respect and protect womanhood. I hope I don't get obnoxious," I lamented.

"No. It's really nice to be treated like I'm something special and not just a piece of property," she said wonderingly.

"I treat every woman like a lady until she proves she's something else. But you: you're special! You're an intelligent woman who also happens to be very lovely and carries herself with grace and aplomb," I pontificated.

"There you go again! Using words and expressions I'd expect from a much older, cultured man."

"You mean I'm not cultured? And what would you say if I told you I was really a seventy-something man, in disguise?" I chuckled.

"I'd say you didn't look your age, or you had a very good plastic surgeon!" she quipped.

"Well, William Clay Hollister's birth certificate says he's only twenty-six, but I had to grow up fast in foster homes, so that may account for me seeming older. Again, I hope it doesn't turn you off," I said apologetically.

"No! It has the opposite effect on me," she replied.

"I'm sorry about that! I've never acted like this around a woman before. I always waited until the second date to even try kissing a girl!" I volunteered.

"It must be the lightning strike!" she said with her cute giggle.

"Maybe, but I get nervous because I feel I'm rushing things with you. I feel I need to stay away so you don't feel pressured," I admitted.

"I don't feel pressured by you! *I've* suggested each time we've been together, except for the first time. You *did* ask me to go to the range, but I suggested we get together afterwards. I'm okay with everything you've done. If I don't like it, you'll know. I can be tactful to warn you. Then, if you don't take the hint, I'll give you both barrels!" she warned.

"Okay, I just didn't want to screw things up. I like you, Izzy; I want to keep in your good graces," I replied.

"Don't worry! Now, are we going to clean those filthy things or not?" she said, all business-like.

It took us about half an hour to clean the three guns. She was much more adept at it than I. She had her first field-stripped and was cleaning it before I even got mine going. She ended up doing the third pistol, and I was done with my first just ahead of her cleaning her second one. Putting everything away and cleaning ourselves up took another fifteen minutes. Finally, she sat on the sofa and waited for me to join her after I went to the refrigerator to get us each a drink. Sitting on opposite ends of the couch, she looked at me over the rim of her glass. Returning her gaze, I would've given a lot to know precisely what she was thinking.

"So, what's up?" I asked her.

"Oh, I was just wondering if I should climb into your lap. There's a lot of space between us," she volunteered.

"That's not a good idea. I may talk like I'm old, but my body reacts like a normal twenty-something."

"What we did before was in public and not a good time for other things. Now, we're in the privacy of your home, and no one is around. Am I making you uncomfortable? Am I acting like a slut?" she asked.

"No, not at all. You're acting like a woman who likes the guy she's with, and I'm flattered!" I answered.

"How do you feel about me? Why don't you show me?" she asked seductively.

Knowing it was foolish, I still couldn't pass up the chance to be intimate with this special woman. Moving down the couch, I took her glass and placed in on the end table.

Kissing her before I embraced her, we had to figure out how to sit together and still kiss. Soon, everything worked out and we spent twenty minutes making out. As I held and caressed her, I tried to transmit through my kisses all the feeling and passion I felt. She was in favor of everything I was doing, and she facilitated my slowly disrobing her. We moved the action to my bedroom, and it was nearly eleven when we lay on my bed, sated and relaxed.

"Thank you, Isabel!" I murmured.

"Thank me? *You*, buster, are one hell of a lover! I've never been with a guy who worked so hard to give me pleasure! And then thanking me? Most guys would have been crowing about their prowess!" She was incredulous.

"But I'm not..." I started.

"I know, 'most guys'! You're sure as hell not! I can't believe I've met the perfect guy!" she gushed.

"I may not be like 'most guys,' but I'm not perfect!" I professed.

"See? You won't even crow about being the perfect lover! I'm so damned glad you like guns!" she exclaimed.

"What?" I gasped.

"Well, if you didn't like guns, you wouldn't have read the poster in the Admin building, and you wouldn't have looked me up, and we wouldn't have been together, and..."

"I get it!" I interrupted.

"Well, I hope so. I also hope you understand I don't end up in bed with a guy within a day or two of meeting him. Yes, it's been a long time for me, but I still don't jump into bed easily. You really make me feel good, and I felt something different from the beginning. I can't explain it!" she confided.

"I feel the same way. I never thought I'd even meet

someone to date for a semester or so. Normally, I'm not very outgoing, and since the accident, I've been even more stand-offish," I explained.

Cuddling for an additional half-hour, we made small talk and just enjoyed being together. I suggested a shower and Isabel thought it was a great idea. We ended up kissing and touching in the shower, but since it was late, we didn't initiate any further play. She saw Bill Hollister's scars on his shoulder and bottoms of his feet. They'd lost most of their ugly redness, so they weren't gross. We dried ourselves and I got to watch her get dressed, since I just threw on some sweats and sneakers. I found myself becoming excited once more but suppressed it. At the front door before we left my place, she pressed herself against me.

"I had a *very* good time! Let's do this again when I don't have to leave," she admitted.

"It was my pleasure. I look forward to a 'sleepover'!" I replied.

Chapter 7

After an early morning run on Wednesday, I drove on campus to meet with the economics professor. I'd brought the textbook Bill had used at his last college. Professor Hadley was familiar with it but didn't consider it equivalent to his course material, which hardly surprised me. We discussed some points of economics where he felt my text was deficient. Again, I was invited to study his own course material and take his final exam. I didn't want to repeat the course, so I took his offer and resigned myself to not only paying for the text but having to study the material. The final exam would be administered the following week on Tuesday. Seeing the handwriting on the wall, I postponed my trip to the bookstore until after my meeting with the math professor that afternoon.

When I had delivered Izzy to her dorm the night before, she had asked me to meet her in the cafeteria at noon again the next day. This time, she wanted to make a formal introduction to her friends. Noon found me walking toward the main cafeteria. I wondered if everyone just allowed the girls to meet at the same table, or whether they had someone arrive early, to stake it out, but no matter, there they were: holding court! I approached the table much like I imagined a courtier did in France or England of the seventeenth or eighteenth century. I felt like bowing and requesting to approach the throne.

It wasn't as though Isabel was haughty about it, but the attitude of other students approached obeisance. The group seemed to take it as their due! Whatever the reason, I felt compelled to deflate them a little. When I was at the table, Isabel introduced me to the others, naming each to me. I acknowledged the introduction.

"So, this is The Gaggle! It's so nice to meet you, ladies."

"What do you mean: gaggle?" asked Cyndee, a petite redhead.

"You didn't know your group was known as The Gaggle by those on campus?"

"No! Why do they call us that?" This from Laurette, a willowy blonde.

"I surmise it's derived from 'girl group' but also because you're always together, like a gaggle of geese, I suppose," I explained.

"Are you being snotty to us?" chirped Cyndee.

"Oh, no! I'm not that way; I was just imparting what I'd heard. There's no rancor. I think you're all held in esteem by your fellow students. You're the 'in group,' and everyone looks up to you for your intelligence and your combined beauty. I wouldn't take the appellation as a denunciation," I solemnly remarked.

"Does he always talk like this, Isabel, or is he trying to impress us with his vocabulary?" This time it was Hilary, a bespectacled, voluptuous brunette.

"Ladies, I don't think Bill is trying to be mean. He's making conversation to get acquainted. Isn't that right, Bill?" Isabel asked.

"To be sure. I've no reason for disrespect toward friends of Isabel. I've only heard good things about you, amidst the obvious envy from the women and longing from the men on campus," I remarked.

"The men don't show it! I feel like a leper! I see lust in their looks, but I've been nearly dateless all year!" complained Rachel, the last of the group to enter the conversation. Rachel was a dark-haired beauty with Eurasian features.

"Well, there's decidedly something wrong with the male student body! It can only be they feel out-classed!" I supplied.

"It didn't seem to bother *you!*" Cyndee, again.

"Isabel was just feeling sorry for the newbie!"

"Knock it off, buster!" Guess who said that?

"Sorry! I just overwhelmed her with my charm and swept her off her feet," I said, grinning.

Isabel gave me a withering look, then immediately changed expressions and sent an 'air kiss' my way.

"You're *almost* insufferable, but I can handle it! Now, we've beat that subject into the ground! We already know we're popular women on campus, but we spend a lot of nights with each other or alone, and not with guys. It's hard to believe they're afraid because we're too popular!" Isabel lamented.

"Let me do some investigation. I'll let you know what I find out," I promised.

Isabel asked me about my appointment with the professor, and I told her about the offer of a final exam. When I mentioned the textbook by name, Hilary said she had the book from a previous semester and would loan it to me. Thanking her, I also mentioned my appointment in the afternoon with the math professor, Professor Ernst. Three of the five had attended one of his classes, and I was asked which class I was challenging. I told them I was aiming to test out of Math 7. Depending on what the outcome of my interview, Rachel had a Math 7 text I could borrow if needed. Happy I was associating with geeks instead of ditzes, I thanked them all for their support.

Taking my arm, and leading me away from the table, Isabel said to her friends: "Be right back, ladies." When we were out of hearing range, Isabel squeezed my arm. "I'd better keep an eye on you, buster!" she teased.

"I won't play around!" I vowed.

"I'm talking about my so-called friends! I could almost hear them panting for you!" she admitted.

"Oh, sure! I doubt that very much," I said skeptically.

"I know my girls. Some of them are so hard up for a date—and the fringe benefits—I wouldn't trust any of them alone with you," she remarked.

"I've never been irresistible to women. And I don't think they'd choose a quickie over your friendship!" I disputed.

"I'm still going to watch you, my naïve boyfriend!" she smilingly told me.

"Am I really your boyfriend?" I asked wonderingly.

"I wouldn't have done what we did last night if you weren't!" she admitted.

"I'm glad! I haven't had a girlfriend since high school," I didn't know anything about Bill's romantic history, but since I didn't, I just went with it!

"You really amaze me! It's as though you just landed on earth, and you're trying to learn how things work. The only reason I don't believe that is because of how you made love to me last night! You've had a lot of practice with *someone!*" she accused.

"Self-help books! They say you can learn anything from books!" I avowed.

"Uh huh! I bet! At least you're discreet! Just don't let me catch you trying to hone your skills with anyone around here, please?" she pleaded. I was surprised to see tears suddenly appear in her eyes. I took her in my arms and hugged her to me.

"I would never hurt you, Iz. I promise!" I whispered into her ear.

Kissing her quickly on the lips, I turned her around and gently propelled her in the direction of her group. Turning back towards me, she blinked the tears away. Then, wiping her cheeks surreptitiously, she gave me a brilliant smile.

"See ya later, Lover! Call or text me at four-thirty, please?" she requested.

"You bet, Izzy! Bye!"

Chapter 8

Professor Ernst was not quite what I'd envisioned, which was a short, stolid, bald man with wire rimmed spectacles. In reality, he was tall and thin with a full head of dark wiry hair. He wore no glasses, but with the way he seemed to squint, he probably wore contacts. He was also younger than I imagined. When we'd made small talk about my background, he began feeling me out, mathematically speaking.

Indicating a problem written on the white board in his office, he asked me if I could describe what I was looking at. I didn't have a degree, but I had taken several classes at a junior college while the Viet Nam Era G.I. Bill was still in effect. One of the classes had been Math 5, which offered an introduction to integral and differential calculus. Because of the class so many years ago and the text Bill had in his apartment, I'd brushed up on my Math 7 skills. Studying the problem on the board, I felt it was familiar. After thinking about it for a couple minutes, I got up from my chair and approached the board. Indicating the dry-erase markers on the tray, I asked:

"May I?"

He nodded his head. So, picking up a contrasting color marker, I went over the mathematical problem in my mind as I followed the equation with the cap-covered tip of the marker. After doing this several times and mumbling to myself, I uncapped the marker and began to solve the equation. I made a couple errors and so went back correcting them. My final solution, I circled and stepped back. Professor Ernst had followed my work but continued to review my solution. Finally, he looked at me.

"Mr. Hollister, the problem on the board was from my final exam *last* semester. It was solved incorrectly by nearly the entire class. I doubt anyone would know to tutor you on that particular equation. So, I must concede you're well founded in the elements of what I teach in Math 7. Consequently, I'm going to offer you a chance to take this semester's final next Thursday, and if you pass, I'll give you credit for the course, and you'll not have to take the class next semester."

"That's very generous of you, Professor! I'd be pleased and grateful to accept your offer to take your final exam. Thank you very much!" I exclaimed.

"Normally, I choose post-graduate students as TAs, but depending on how you do on the final, I wonder if you'd be interested in being a TA for me next semester?" he queried.

"I'm very flattered, sir! What will your students think if they find out I'm an undergrad?" I uttered.

"If the Department Head approves my choices, they've nothing to say about it. I'd only require you to teach one or two classes during the semester, but I feel confident in your abilities. What do you say, Mr. Hollister?" Professor Ernst asked.

"I'd be happy to assist you, Professor. Thank you for the opportunity."

"You're welcome! I'll send an email to Admin, so they can schedule you for the exam."

"Thank you, sir!" I gushed.

"Take care, Mr. Hollister. Please see me at the beginning of the semester," he advised.

"Will do, Professor."

I was astonished I had pulled it off. One math problem! I knew I'd been extremely fortunate; almost any other equation may have stumped me. I wanted to tell Isabel but had nearly two hours before I could call her. I decided to walk by the Mall, to see if her, or any one of The Gaggle were there. I saw Rachel and Hilary sitting on a bench, so I approached them.

"Afternoon, ladies! Do you know where Isabel would be about now?" I asked.

"Oh, hello, Bill! Let's see... she's probably in her French class. Her last one for the day. It just started," Rachel volunteered.

"Oh, okay! Thanks," I replied.

"How did your conference go with Professor Ernst?"

"He was extremely generous. He gave me an oral exam to check my comprehension and then invited me to take the semester final! So... I guess I'll need to borrow your Math 7 book after all. Thanks for the offer, Rachel!" I reported.

"You're welcome. I'll get the book to you," Rachel replied.

Hilary broke in: "Oh, yeah! Do you want to get that economics book now?"

"I might as well. I have some time to wait, before I can see Isabel," I admitted.

"Come with me to my dorm, and I'll get it for you," she offered.

Hilary was not in the same dorm as Isabel, but hers was co-ed, so I wasn't even looked at twice as I entered the building. Hilary took me up to the fourth floor, and I followed her down the hallway. At her door, she said:

"Don't mind the mess! My roommate's a slob!"

Opening the door, she went in, and I followed. Leaving the door open, I stepped a few feet inside the door, being very conscious of being in a private room with an attractive woman.

"Oh, come on in! I'm not going to bite you!"

Opening her closet, she began rummaging, first on the shelf, then on the floor in the back. While she was bent over, she showed a great deal of her thighs and at a couple points her skirt rose to reveal her crotch, which was just barely covered by a thong. I averted my eyes, trying not to take advantage of the view. After five minutes of searching, she backed out of the closet and stood up. As she turned towards me, she had a book in her hand. I noticed she glanced down at my pants. I could feel a slight tightness there. Bringing the book, she came right up to me, put her arms around me, and hugged me against her voluptuous form.

"Did you see anything you wanted to see more of?" Hilary asked.

"Uh, Hilary, I don't think this is a good idea!"

"Bill, you've got Izzy so crazy for you, you've got to be a stud! I'm soooo horny. Can't you spread yourself to more than one woman?"

"I'm pretty sure Isabel wouldn't agree to something like that. You're a very attractive woman, and if I wasn't with Isabel, you'd be lying on the bed, with me showing you how much a stud I could be, but I won't hurt Isabel," I said adamantly.

"But I can feel you pressing it against me!" Hilary whined.

"My body has a mind of its own, but right now, the brain in my big head won't let me do anything with you!" I excused.

"Oh, Bill! You're so mean to me! Maybe I should tell Iz how you came on to me, and I had to fight you off!" Hilary threatened.

"No, you won't, you slut!" came the sound of Rachel's voice.

Turning around and pulling Hilary around with me, I saw Rachel standing in the doorway. I had left the door open for propriety, and I was glad I did! Hilary backed away from me, looking down once more at the front of my pants. Rachel saw it too but continued to dress Hilary down.

"I thought you seemed awful eager to get him up to your dorm just to give him a stupid textbook! I thought I'd see what you were up to. I saw you flaunting your goodies at him, bent over way too far, in the closet! I heard everything! You should have your eyes scratched out for trying to steal Izzy's man!" Rachel boomed.

"Aw, I didn't want to keep him! I just wanted to borrow him for a little while. I would've cleaned him up good and sent him back to Isabel, and if I know men, he wouldn't have told! I must be losing my touch. I usually don't strike out, once I get a man in a room alone. I just haven't been able to do that recently! I'm sorry, Bill! I guess I've really screwed things up! Are you going to tell on me, Rachel?" Hilary sobbed.

"I don't want Isabel to know anything about this. Luckily nothing happened. Bill, you're stronger than I imagined a man could be, and I'm glad I can vouch for your fidelity, with the way she was starting to blackmail you. If you ever try to say anything about this, Hilary, I'll tell everything. Now, Bill, take the damned book and get out of here. Go home, and call Isabel at four-thirty like she asked. Take care of that thing in your pants too, or save it for Izzy, the lucky girl! I'm going to stay here and talk to Hilary some more!" Rachel strongly advised.

So, I got the hell out of there and didn't slow down until I was in the privacy and safety of my home. Not surprisingly, I'd deflated and felt my male parts had betrayed me! I had to admit, however, any of The Gaggle could have evoked that kind of response, dammit! I really didn't want to hurt Isabel, so I vowed to never get into a situation like that again!

Taking stock of what was available to cook; I decided to start something I could share with Isabel if she wanted to take potluck. I ended up thawing some steaks and putting them in a marinade I whipped up. By then, it was a little after four-thirty, so I grabbed my phone and called. Answering her phone on the first ring, she seemed glad to hear from me.

After a few words of endearment, she said: "We should begin studying for the history final."

I invited her over for dinner, then offered to take her someplace she felt safe from ravishment, so we could study. She laughed.

"I feel safe at your place, as we already have a deal to be serious about our study time," she replied.

"But we made the deal before we became intimate," I observed.

"I trust you!" she told me.

Rats! I offered to come pick her up, but she said she'd run herself over, so I wouldn't need to leave home so late. She said she'd be over within the hour, so I started my new BBQ grill. When she arrived, I was putting the finishing touches on our salads, and had baked potatoes in the microwave. While I put the steaks on, she set the table. Dinner was great, largely due to the company! We had iced tea to drink, and she really liked the way I'd grilled the steaks, talking long after the meal was consumed.

"You know, this is the first time I've ever gotten domestic with a boyfriend," she remarked. According to her, they usually ate out or expected her to cook something for them. This had proven difficult, as she had no cooking facilities at school and any boyfriend she had had in the last four years was either in a dorm also or lived with his parents. Feeling like she was really grown up, now she had a boyfriend who had his own place in town! We laughed about it. She admitted our relationship was so very different from anything she'd ever had. We cleaned up together, and then set our study materials on the kitchen table. Then, we got down to serious studying.

Isabel had a great grasp of history, and more to the point, she had an uncanny insight into how the professor thought about the various events in history, and this was also verified by the way the events were covered in the textbook. Of course, we couldn't accomplish all the study in one evening, so agreed we needed an additional evening of study. At the completion of our 'cram session,' I told her about my conference with Professor Ernst. She was thrilled with the outcome. I also reminded her of my need to study for my economics and math finals. For economics, there was no known study partner, so I was on my own. It was nearly midnight before we called it quits. Although she'd driven to my place in her own car, I insisted on following her back on campus, and seeing she made it from her parking area to her dorm, without any problems. I jumped out of my car at the curb in front of Blanton Dormitory and gave her a lingering kiss, before standing and watching her enter the building. I then drove back home.

Chapter 9

Thursday after my run, I worked in my yard, getting it cut, trimmed, and swept. There were very few flowers, but the lawn and shrubs needed trimming. It looked a lot better when I was finished. Isabel knew I wouldn't be coming on campus that day. She had given me a sad face when I told her and asked me to call her at four-thirty, anyway. I spent the afternoon studying economics and remembered to call Professor Taggert's secretary to sign up for the history final. Like a good boyfriend, I called her at four-thirty on the dot! Telling me she'd missed me at lunch, Izzy asked if she could come over for a short visit. I told her to come over anytime. Half an hour later, she knocked on my door. When I opened it, she pushed me inside, and back onto the couch, where she straddled my legs and bent over me for a long, drawn-out kiss. She *had* missed me!

Two hours later, we took another shower together to wash off the perspiration and other body fluids. It was a little late, but I questioned her about birth control. She teared-up a little and thanked me for being concerned and responsible. Although she was wearing an IUD, she had needed it very little in the last couple years, but had kept it current, just in case. After drying off, she pulled me back to bed. She told me then, the reason for her visit.

"You, sweetie, are being rewarded!" she admitted.

The Gaggle had been at lunch, and it was apparent there was a problem. Hilary and Rachel were acting weird, so they were ganged-up on by the other three, and the whole story about Hilary and me came out. Rachel told the story, with protestations from Hilary. Afterwards, each of the other three women cross-examined the two, and it was agreed Hilary would be punished in a manner to be determined, and I was to be rewarded. Isabel had made no bones about who was giving out the reward, although she had volunteers to help. Laying in my arms, she said:

"Thank you, so very much, Bill. I appreciate it, from the bottom of my heart!" Then she kissed me very tenderly. We then dressed and went out for a burger.

Stating she had no classes on Friday, Isabel asked if we could devote at least four hours to studying history. I agreed, and we decided to make it early, so we could do something fun in the afternoon. Meeting at the campus library, Izzy and I were very committed to our studies! At the end of the pre-determined four hours, we decided one more study session would do us good, and we agreed to make it Tuesday, after my economics final was done. This left me a couple days free to study for economics on my own. I knew I would have Saturday morning free because Isabel had a firearms competition.

Not really being free to just tour around the city, we decided to drive around a while, and then go to the Austin Zoo. It was a fun way to spend a couple hours, and then I took her out to dinner. There were a lot of places we could have gone, if we'd wanted to go home and get dressed up, but there were plenty of places to go as we were! South Texas BBQ was always one of my favorites, so we found a place we'd heard about from people we struck up a conversation with while at the zoo. The place was noisy, but the food was great! I took Isabel back to her dorm around ten p.m.

Parking my car in front of the dorm, I walked her to the front door, where she gave me a sweet kiss and said good-night. She asked me to call her around two in the afternoon the next day. As I walked toward my car, a group of three guys were heading in my direction. Figuring they were there to pick up a date, it didn't really occur to me it was awful late to begin a date. My mind was on other things, so I didn't realize they had blocked my way on the sidewalk. Becoming aware my progress was impeded, I looked up and saw the three men. The obvious leader spoke:

"You seem awfully friendly with Isabel. You doin' her?"

"It's none of your business what I do with whomever. Isabel is a good friend."

"I'll bet she really gets down and dirty, the little tramp!"

"I'd watch what you say about my friend, dummy!"

"I've invested a lot of time these last two years making sure no guy dates her. I've also discouraged anyone dating her whore friends, too!"

"Why would you even bother doing that?"

"Because the bitch wouldn't date me again, after I showed her how a real man treats his slut-whore!"

"You must be a misogynist!"

"I'm not any kind of miss! I'm a man!"

"A woman hater!"

"I don't hate women as long as they act like they should!"

"Only an animal treats a woman like a piece of meat! You really need your balls cut off!" I threatened.

"I think that's what me and the boys will do to you!" he snarled.

Realizing I was about to get my butt kicked three to one, I didn't wait. Deciding to get my licks in first, I kicked the one on my right square in the crotch. He immediately folded up and began rolling around on the ground, holding himself, and the knife in his hand clattered to the cement. Pivoting to my left, I tried to set myself, but the leader swung a blow at my head. Not being quick enough to totally avoid the punch, I took a hit to the side of my right eye, near my temple. It stung like hell, and I saw stars.

By the time my head cleared, I saw the leader had stepped back and was preparing to attack again. I took the initiative to punch the guy on my far left in the nose. As he brought both hands up to grab his now broken nose, the knife in his hand cut his chin. This left me facing the man who'd threatened me.

"Let's see what you've got, woman hater!" I invited.

With a snarl, he swung on me again. I ducked under the swing, but he elbowed me in the head, on his backswing. I grunted and saw stars again as I stumbled. This gave the guy on my left the chance to bring his knife into play, and I tried to avoid it. At this time, the leader pushed me toward his knife wielding crony, and the knife sliced into the meat of my bicep. I knew I was hurt, now, but tried to avoid further injury by backing away from the trio. The one on my right had stopped rolling around and holding his crotch, so he decided he wanted a piece of me, and picked his knife back up. Holding my cut arm, I danced away from him and tripped. This gave the other two the chance to kick at me. Taking a couple blows to the ribs and legs, I tried to fend them off with my own kicks while on my back. They were now circling me, like a pack of wolves, waiting for a chance to attack.

I rolled over and got to my feet just in time to be rushed by all three. I felt a couple more stabs from the knives and was hit in the head again on the right side. The leader tried to kick me, so I grabbed his foot and lifted. This action caused him to hop on his left leg to maintain his balance, but I shoved him with the foot I was holding, and he fell to his back. The other two, with their knives, were trying to bring them to bear, when they saw a security guard rushing toward us. They immediately dropped their knives and backed off.

Suddenly, we were joined by a uniformed security guard. He had a nightstick and was threatening to wield it if we didn't stop. I was breathing deeply and could feel the sting on the side of my head and pain from my many cuts. Putting a hand to the area on my head, it came back with a little blood on it. I noticed then; the leader wore an ornate ring on the hand he hit me with. He, himself, was now standing and panting, but still game, casting ugly looks my way. His cohorts flanked him, one trying to stanch the flow of blood from his nose and the other crouching over to reduce the pain from his crotch, as the security guard began asking questions and taking notes. I suddenly wondered where in the hell I had learned the moves I used. Fred Lambson had never had a fight as an adult, though he'd been an avid fan of martial arts movies. Were there some residual memories of fighting left over in my brain, from the original Bill Hollister? I could only wonder. The actual fight had taken about a minute and a half, and had seemed reflexive or automatic, although I had come away worse for the wear.

When it was my turn to answer the security guards' questions, I did so succinctly. I didn't have a student body I.D. but told the guard Admin office would vouch for me being authorized to be on campus. I didn't bring Isabel's name into it. I also learned my attackers' names. Ben Huntley was the leader; his henchmen were Marty Holcomb and Randy Miller. I didn't hear their statements, but the guard told us he'd watched part of the altercation before he could break it up. Getting the guard's permission to leave, I went to my car and drove off.

At home, I took stock of my injuries. The cut on my arm was not deep but had bled some. The other stab wounds were superficial and had only bled a little, but I figured the bruises from the kicks would begin to show tomorrow. So, I took a quick shower, to remove the dirt and debris from the ground. Once dried off, I put a couple butterfly bandages on my arm to hold it shut, and then put anti-bacterial salve and band-aids on the stab wounds and the cut on my temple. After that, I went to bed.

Chapter 10

The ringing of my phone woke me the next morning. With my voice full of sleep, I think I articulated: "Hello?"

"Bill, this is Isabel! Sorry to wake you!" Without waiting, she continued, "I know you may not feel like it, but will you do me a favor? One of the members of my shooting team was just called home due to a death in the family, and they're packing as we speak. I need a fill-in at the competition and can't contact anyone on my back-up roster," she cried.

"Sure, Isabel. I can do it," I volunteered, knowing I was hurting.

I had to be there in less than an hour, and she'd given me directions to the meet range, absently reminding me to bring my pistols. Ammunition was provided by the club, which was a good thing, because stopping to buy ammo would make me late. Jumping out of bed, I was reminded of the beating I'd taken last night, but I decided against another shower and just washed the sleep from my face and put on clothes. Within fifteen minutes, I was in my car. I felt like crap, I needed a cup of coffee, and I wouldn't turn down breakfast. I settled for a cup of coffee and a doughnut, from a convenience store and had it drank before I showed up at the meet!

Arriving at the competition site, I was met as I got out of my car by Isabel and three other members of her team, one being Tim Latham. Giving me a quick hug and kiss, she thanked me for coming to her rescue. Glancing at my head and the band-aid, I expected her to ask about it, but she said nothing. Chalking it up to being too busy with the meet to be distracted, I just grabbed my gun tote from the seat of the car and followed her to our staging area. Being introduced to the others, the team was made up of Isabel; myself; Tim; another guy, Greg; and another woman, Michelle. I was the oldest, with Isabel being next. I was given a quick rundown on the schedule and the routine. It was my first real competition, I was nervous, and my right hand and arm were stiff from the fight.

My place in the shooting schedule made me fourth, behind Isabel, Greg, and then Michelle. Following me, as clean up, was Tim. Being glad I was not first, I watched intently those who went before me. Isabel was calm, as I expected her to be. Greg and Michelle were nervous but made a good showing. When my turn came, I acted like this was old stuff and managed to appear calm, although I had a headache and my hands and arm were stiff. I took my time with my firing, except during the timed firing. The meet consisted of eight teams, and it went for three rounds, with the winner being the team with the highest cumulative score.

When the standings were posted, we were in first place, my own totals score just ten points behind Isabel. The whole team went nuts! This was their first time taking high score. Isabel told me the person I had replaced was usually their low scorer, and my much higher numbers may have spurred the others to do their very best. The trophies were awarded, and the group wanted to celebrate by going someplace for lunch. I offered to buy, since I was the new guy. After lunch, Isabel followed me home.

Once inside, Izzy sat me down on the couch and peeled off my band-aid, then gently removed my shirt to examine my arm and other wounds. Kissing my head wound, she re-marked: "Well, Mr. Tough Guy, what are you going to do for an encore?"

"You know about what happened last night?" I moaned.

"Yes. I not only heard all about it, but I've got a copy of the whole thing on video!"

"What? You're kidding me!" I exclaimed.

"No! One of the girls, a film major, with a room over-looking the front, was practicing technique with her digital movie camera. She got our good night kiss on video too, by the way! Anyway, she kept the camera rolling as you walked away, and she caught the interchange between you and those assholes. She had a parabolic microphone pointed in the same direction, so she picked up every word, including what Ben Huntley said to his kiss-ass sidekicks before they confronted you."

"I hope you're not disappointed in me. I don't want to cause you any problems," I pleaded.

"Disappointed? Oh no, my dear. I'm pleased as the prover-bial punch! Not only did you give the bastards a beating, but you solved the mystery of why I and my group were being ignored by the so-called men on campus. To think Ben and his entourage were warning all the guys to stay away from my group, especially me. It's so unbelievable, until you consider the kind of bastard Ben Huntley turned out to be. I dated him a couple times when I was a freshman. On the second date, he all but raped me! I was sore for days after he got through with me, and I refused to be alone with him again! I almost took my gun and blew his crotch off, but he wasn't worth it. Now, I have a hero, and I find myself continually amazed at how sweet and kind you are to me. To top it all off, you left your nice warm bed to come to my rescue this morning and helped us take first place. I feel I need to reward you, somehow, but I suppose giving you my body is nothing new!" she lamented.

Taking her in my arms and kissing her tenderly, I said: "Isabel, your body will always be new and exciting to me. My belief is everyone, especially women, have full rights to their minds and bodies, and no one should have the right to subjugate either, without the express permission of the individual. What that means is you are the only one who can give permission for anyone to touch, kiss, or otherwise make use of your sweet self. I'd never take for granted the right to make love to you and would expect you to *allow* me access every time. If I'd had my way in the fight last night, I would have possibly killed or maimed for life that poor excuse of a man! I have very strong feelings about how rapists or abusers of women should be punished. Unfortunately, our current laws will not allow to happen what I believe is justified. Just being in your presence is reward enough for me, Izzy. In fact, let me make dinner for you or take you someplace you really want to go for dinner!"

"What I want to do first is clean our weapons! Then, I think tonight should be a sleepover! I'll need to go back to the dorm to pack a small bag, but I'll come right back. Then, we'll do whatever comes to mind, the rest of the day. I want to make you breakfast tomorrow, then go back to bed and cuddle for a long time. We don't have to make love, unless you want to, but I want to be in your arms as much as possible tomorrow."

"That sounds like a heavenly reward to me, except for the gun cleaning, but I know it's necessary!" I admitted.

Our weekend went just as Isabel wanted it to go! We did go out for dinner on Saturday, but we stayed in the rest of the time. Being conservative about it, we paced our self in our lovemaking. We talked a good bit and watched a movie. I got at least two solid hours of economics study accomplished while Izzy took a nap cuddled up to me in bed. I managed to get a run in while Izzy fixed us a light meal. Late in the evening on Sunday, I nearly had to shove Isabel out the door so she could go back to her dorm and get prepared for her Monday morning class. I don't remember Fred having this much enjoyment, but maybe it was just selective memory!

Chapter 11

At eight-thirty on Monday, I got a call from the Dean's office requesting I meet with him at ten that morning. I wasn't sure, but I had a feeling it was about my fisticuffs on Friday! I took a chance Isabel would still be in her room, and I lucked out! I told her about my suspicions and asked if I could get a copy of the video she had. She was just on her way out the door, but would leave it with Cyndee, who would meet me at the Dean's office. Arriving at ten minutes before ten, I found Cyndee waiting for me. After handing me the disk, she gave me a quick kiss on my cheek thanking me for my discovery and wishing me luck.

Precisely at ten, I was ushered into the Dean's office, which could also be used as a conference room. I saw my antagonists were already present. The Dean opened:

"Mr. Hollister, we haven't met before since you're quite new here. I believe you know these three gentlemen, perhaps not by name, but you've had contact with them!"

I gave the three a cold stare, and the smirks on their faces told me they thought they had everything under control. The Dean continued:

"I refer to the alleged attack you perpetrated on these younger men last Friday evening. They say you attacked them after you refused them access to Blanton Dormitory, where they had dates with some young women. I've heard their side of things. Now, I give you equal opportunity to present your side of the story."

"Dean, I'd be wasting my time presenting a subjective rebuttal to their pack of lies! Why don't we hear an objective view? There should be a report of the incident in Campus Security. I know a guard took statements, and he witnessed the event from a short distance away," I replied formally.

"What? Security was present, you say?" the Dean sputtered. He was already fumbling for the phone on his desk. Dialing a number, he spoke for a moment, then listened for a couple more, and then spoke again. Hanging up the phone, he addressed us as a group: "Security *does* have an incident report, and also the officer who took your statements is on his way over."

Ben Huntley spoke: "Dean, our statements will agree with what we told you, but the rent-a-cop on duty will probably side with Hollister. Security has it in for me and my friends!"

"We'll wait and see what the officer has to say!" the Dean replied.

So, we sat and waited for ten minutes or so until the security guard who'd been there on Friday came in the door. Handing the Dean a couple sheets of paper, we waited until the Dean could review the incident report.

"Okay, I've read the report. Now, Officer Tanner, please tell me what you witnessed," requested the Dean.

"Well, Dean, I was making my rounds in the vicinity of Blanton—we patrol it pretty often, to make sure the women are safe—and I saw the guy over there, uh, Mr. Hollister, I believe, walking a young woman to the door. They, uh, kissed good night, and then Mr. Hollister walked back toward his car. I'd noticed the other three walking around, then watching Mr. Hollister and the young lady drive up and... do what they did.

"When Mr. Hollister headed for his car, these three blocked his way and I heard them talking, but I didn't hear what was being said. Suddenly, I saw Hollister kick... him in the balls, uh, the crotch! He fell to the ground and Hollister and Huntley began punching each other. Then Hollister hit the other one, over there, in the nose and he was holding it and moaning. There was all kinds of blood coming out between his fingers. Then, Hollister said something to Mr. Huntley, and Mr. Huntley took another swing. It all kind of went too fast to really describe after that, but it ended with Hollister on the ground for a second, with the others circling him. Then Hollister stood up and faced them. When I came up to them, there were two knives on the ground. No one claimed them, so I put them in the evidence locker," concluded the officer.

"Thank you, Officer Tanner. Do you think Mr. Hollister initiated the attack?"

"Well, he sure got in the first kick, but it could have been something they said to him."

"Thank you for your input. That will be all!" The Dean said dismissively. The officer left and the Dean turned to me. "Was it something they said which caused you to viciously attack these men?"

"Dean, we could take all day with 'he said/he said': my word against theirs. What we need is some totally objective testimony," I suggested.

"That would be ideal, young man, but there are no more witnesses," responded the Dean.

"Dean, this university has some excellent departments for a number of majors. One of those is your film school. What Mr. Huntley, Mr. Miller, and Mr. Holcomb were unaware of was a student in that film school was practicing her camera skills on Friday night, and she had the camera trained on the front of the dormitory. I have with me a completely unbiased and unedited account of the event we're discussing. Do you have a video player in your office?" I asked.

"Excellent! Yes! There's a video player in that wall cabinet. Would you please show us the video?" said the Dean excitedly. My antagonists turned white.

During the viewing, the Dean was visibly disturbed by what he saw. The part I had not known about was what Ben had said before he confronted me. Here's an approximation of his remarks to Miller and Holcomb:

"Look! There's that bitch-whore Isabel Grey! We haven't had to run anyone off for a while, so we should make it good. I hate that damned slut and all her whore friends. I think we need to show this guy we mean business, so get out your knives. We aren't gonna kill him, but we'll make him bleed a little and he'll pass the word to leave Grey and her Gaggle alone! Here he comes..."

The video picked up all the lies they were telling the security guard too! When it ended, there was complete quiet in the room for the space of a minute. Then the Dean began again.

"So, uh 'gentlemen,' I see you've come to me with such spurious claims that I've a mind to throw you out of this school immediately. Since we're so close to the end of semester, I'll allow you to finish your finals, but then I strongly encourage you to withdraw and seek to further your education at some other institution. Is there anything additional anyone feels is germane to the issue?"

"Look, Dean, my father won't like this. He donates a lot of money to this place! I'll call him and..."

"Mr. Huntley, I suggest you shut the hell up! If you decide to approach your father to complain about your treatment, I will send your father a copy of the incident report, the video, and my own opinion of your contemptible behavior. Is that clear? Mr. Holcomb, I believe you're here on a scholarship. It's regrettable, but your choice of companions will cause your scholarship to be withdrawn. You three are excused! Mr. Hollister, a word, if you please?" the Dean finished.

When the door to the office closed, the Dean approached me and held out his hand. Taking it in mine, we shook hands.

"Mr. Hollister: First, I want to extend a sincere apology to you for this incident. It may put you off wanting to attend our institution, but I hope not. Second, I want to commend you on your handling of your defense, both on Friday night and here in this office. You're very astute and well-spoken. I wonder why you're pursuing a degree in math. You'd be an asset to the legal profession. Third, I'm appalled such a conspiracy of intimidation has been taking place under my nose, presumably for the last two years! I'm grateful you uncovered it, and now maybe the young women who were the victims can have some peace of mind, and a much better social life. It won't take long for the word to get out. We have a very effective rumor mill, but apparently a strong code of silence on certain matters too!

"I understand you've been successful in your quest for credits by challenging some courses. I wish you luck on the finals this week. I hope you decide to stay and enroll for next semester. I already feel you'll be an asset to our student body, and may I encourage you to seek a position in our student government, as well! Is there anything I can do for you, Mr. Hollister?" he concluded.

"No, you've been very understanding and fair. It will be up to me to succeed in my endeavors to earn my degree from your school. I've found some good friends in my short time here and look forward to making many more. However, I want you to understand I'm seriously seeking my degree, and I'm not here for the social aspect of campus life. It is merely incidental to life in general."

"I applaud your dedication to academic pursuits. My door is always open to students. Now, if you'll excuse me, I have a budget meeting to attend. Have a good day, Mr. Hollister."

"Good day, Dean."

Walking out of the Admin building, I could but wonder whether the Dean's degree had been in law. The way he'd conducted the meeting made me feel I'd been in a courtroom. The only thing missing had been a bailiff to administer the oath! It was now a little after eleven, so I had roughly an hour to kill until I could see Isabel in the cafeteria. I was about to get in my car and take a quick trip home when I was hailed. It was Izzy, Cyndee, and Laurette. Coming my way, I waited until they got to me. Each was grinning and had flushed faces.

"The man of the hour!" Cyndee chirped.

Isabel stood back while each woman gave me a hug and a chaste kiss, then she moved in for an enhanced show of affection.

"How did it go with the Dean? Did the video help?"

"The video was the 'smoking gun,' and it sealed their doom, as they had concocted a tale of woe, making me the aggressor and a monster. The security guard cast some doubts on their story, but the movie, especially what they said before they accosted me, was the real clincher. Now, they're toast! They can finish their finals, but they won't be able to come back next semester!"

All three women were jumping up and down, clapping their hands. Alliteration would say it thus: the bevy of bouncing breasts was beautiful beyond belief! Gushing with enthusiasm, they were all trying to talk over each other. Then there were two more females hugging and kissing me, and The Gaggle was complete! When things calmed down, we went to the main cafeteria. As we entered, there was a round of applause accorded me, causing me to turn every hue of red possible for the human complexion. Isabel remarked:

"Awww, you're so cute! Too bad elections for student body president are over. You'd win by a landslide!"

When the clamoring subsided, we sat at the traditional table. I was asked what I wanted to eat, and then girls from The Gaggle argued about who would get it, and who would pay for it! It was difficult to remember I was at college. It felt more like high school! Lunch ended up being a raucous affair, and there were a few visits from young men asking the girls out. Isabel turned down a dozen invitations before she grabbed my hand and we left.

On the way out, I quipped: "Maybe you should stick around. Perhaps a better offer will come along."

Isabel gave me a withering look and said: "Don't piss me off, Bill. It's been a great morning, so don't ruin it!"

So, I walked her back to her dorm, where she invited me in for the first time. Her roommate was Cyndee, and they kept a pretty nice room. Against my better judgment, I let her pull me onto her bed. Because she had a class at one-thirty, I wouldn't let our making out go too far. She pouted for a while but understood the wisdom of not getting too mussed. At one-fifteen, we left the dorm and I walked her to her class, and then told her I needed to study for my economics final. We agreed to meet tomorrow at noon, as usual.

Studying until late into the evening, I was in bed by eleven, so I could get a good night's sleep. The economics final was at ten in the morning, so I was up early, to get a run in before showering and dressing. I was in the classroom by nine-forty-five. When Professor Hadley walked in, he noticed me and acknowledged my presence. He didn't waste time and handed out the exam booklets. Noting the time, he told us we had two hours and the booklets would be on his desk at precisely twelve-oh-five! Normally, I'm good at taking tests, especially if they're 'completion,' or 'multiple choice,' but Professor Hadley liked essay questions. I can BS my way through most subjects, but economics was not so easy for me. Fortunately, the material was fresh in my mind, so I figured I did well. Finished well before noon, I just reviewed my answers, making sure I made no glaring grammatical errors, and handed the booklet in by eleven-forty-five.

Walking into the cafeteria, I received a lot of greetings, or at least smiles. I had no idea who they all were, but they knew who I was! It's amazing: in one week I went from a complete unknown to a major topic of discussion on campus. It was a bit unsettling! The Gaggle was again holding court, but now with many more courtiers. Isabel was holding herself aloof, and when she saw me, she came toward me.

"How was the exam?" Isabel enquired.

"I did okay, I guess. It'll depend on how he grades it. How was your morning?"

"Fine, but I missed you. Are we still studying together tonight?" She asked, with questioning eyebrows.

"I'm looking forward to it." I answered.

"Me too! I've no class this afternoon, so we could get started early, if you want."

"You're talking 'study,' right?" And I heard her cute giggle.

"Of course! What else could I want from you?" she said, smiling mischievously.

"Dinner, maybe?" I queried.

"Yeah, that's it! How about some finger foods so we don't have to stop and fix a meal?" she suggested.

"Good idea!" I agreed.

Because study was important to both of us, we had a successful session. Being all business, other than occasional winks and smiles, we covered what material we felt pertinent. By ten o'clock, we'd closed our books and Izzy's notes and sat on the couch discussing what we believed he would ask on the exam. I was walking her to the front door of the dormitory by eleven. Kissing her, and bidding her a good sleep, I told her I'd see her in class.

The next morning, Isabel was waiting for me outside the history building and greeted me warmly. By now, people knew we were a couple, and our kissing in public had become the norm. Going inside and finding a place to sit, we sat a couple rows apart, so no one could accuse us of cheating. The other students drifted in and when the class began, nearly all the seats were filled. The exam itself was a multimedia affair, with pictures of historical figures and sites to identify. Methods used to administer this exam were decidedly different, and I was surprised. That said, I still felt I did well. Since the pace was regulated by the media-driven material, most everyone finished at the same time. Walking to the front to hand in my booklet, Professor Taggert asked me what I thought of his exam. Remarking how it was different than I'd seen before, he took it as a compliment. He wished me luck. Isabel was right behind me, so we walked out together.

"How was it, Iz?" I inquired.

"I think I did pretty well, and our study sessions helped a lot."

"I agree, and I think I did all right, too. What now? Do you want to go meet your friends?"

"Sure! I think there may be a few more pairings for our group, unless I'm mistaken! Hilary's made a conquest, and he's a junior. He follows her around like a puppy, but she's really happy! Cyndee was out late last night and has a final this afternoon, so she may not be at lunch. She regretted not spending last night studying. Rachel and Laurette haven't been on dates yet, but they've been talking to a couple different guys. If things go much further, The Gaggle may cease to exist, in its present form, but that's not a bad thing... right?" Isabel asked.

"Things don't remain the same. You're all seniors, and with only one more semester after this one, you'll be splitting up anyway! I'm not being callous, just realistic. Of course, some will continue toward their Masters, but some will enter the work force and not have time for campus life. It's just *life*! I guess the thing foremost in my mind is: what will happen between you and me? I know we've only known each other for a week and a half, but a lot happened in that time. Before I came here, I didn't think I'd even date until I'd been here a few months. Meeting you was a totally unexpected pleasure."

"Sweet-talker! For me, the way things have been the last two years, I was resigned to not having a relationship until I was out of here, and working on my MS. I was completely surprised you were so easy to like and get to know. I guess I *was* a man-hater, of sorts, after all! I may have missed some nice guys because of Ben's little conspiracy!"

"I don't like it, but I should give you a chance to find out!"

"Uh uh! I'm not giving up the bird in the hand! You're stuck with me, buster, unless you want to look around. I did get you as soon as you stepped on campus!"

"Not me, gorgeous! I know I'm not going to find anyone else as great as you!"

"Okay, you've been sweet-talkin' me long enough! Take me home and show me how much you love me, please?"

"As you wish, Princess Isabel!"

For me, my abbreviated semester was nearly over with just my math final to go, but Isabel had three more finals. At their completion, we spent nearly all our time together. During semester break, we took a trip to Corpus Christi and stayed at a motel for a week, spending our days at the beach. By the time we got back, the grades were out. Isabel had always been a good student and made good grades. I earned a '3.0' in economics, and a '4.0' in history and math.

Though we had different majors—Isabel's was for a BS in engineering—we had looked for classes we could take together next semester. My fear of being too close too fast became a reality. We'd been drifting along, living in the moment, but we both knew we'd be separating at the end of the semester when Isabel transferred to New England to work on her Masters at MIT. I was at least committed to remaining at UTA to complete my BS and, loathe to relocate again, would most likely stay at UTA for my Masters. I tried not to think about it, but the thought of losing Isabel was gut-wrenching.

Izzy maintained her dorm room, but when the semester began, she spent most nights at my house. By mid-semester, that changed in that we weren't spending so much time together, with her spending more nights at the dorm. We weren't fighting, but her independent nature caused her to feel stifled. To my knowledge, there was no one else for either of us. We just felt our studies were more important than our relationship, which was not a bad thing. By finals week we hadn't slept together in a week, and though we still were close friends, the white-hot nature of our beginning had cooled. We spent time discussing the merits of maintaining a long-distance relationship and pledged to keep it alive, but the end seemed inevitable to me. She would move on, and it was excruciating to admit.

At semester's end and Isabel's graduation, I gave her a going away party, which was well attended by her friends. She'd be going home to visit her parents before going on to MIT. Deep down, I felt an abiding love for this intelligent, beautiful woman but was reluctant to make a commitment that could distract her and hold her back. After the party was over, I took her back to the dorm so she could complete her packing. At the front door, I decided to make the break as we said our goodbyes.

"Isabel, I want you to know I'll always cherish our relationship! I never thought I could be so happy. I probably got on your nerves, so I hope you find someone at MIT who won't. I know you'll be busy, but please send me an email now and then, to let me know how you're doing. If your boyfriend gets jealous, just tell him I'm some old guy you struck up a friendship with and that I'm harmless!" I tried to be jovial, but my insides were tied in knots.

"Bill, you make it sound so final. I'm just going there for school. It won't take forever, and we can then be back together," she said confidently.

"If there's anything I can do for you, just ask. I'll do it in a heartbeat!" I remarked sadly.

"Oh, Bill, don't be that way. You've been the sweetest guy I've ever known. Kind, generous, and a great lover! We'll meet again, after we have our degrees, and revisit 'Us.' I'll never forget you, and I'll stay in touch. I've a feeling there are a number of women waiting for me to leave, so they can pounce!"

She was barely containing her composure, and I was close to crying too!

"I doubt it! I was so lucky to meet you when I did. You'll forever be in my heart. Please take care! Good luck, Ms. Isabel Grey."

Giving her a soft, lingering kiss, I then stepped back and turned away, so she couldn't see the tears beginning to run down my face. I heard her reply: "Thank you, William Clay Hollister! Bye."

Chapter 12

During the semester break, I ran a lot and shot up a lot of ammo to let off steam. I turned down the presidency of the Firearms Club because my heart wouldn't really be in it without Isabel. I attended the matches, when scheduled, so it was a minor inconvenience. My morosity was palpable. I knew I loved Isabel but didn't have the courage to tell her, which made me castigate myself regularly. At the same time, I was driven to succeed—as Bill Hollister—to prove I could do it, given a second chance. I was angry I'd let myself become involved with someone so early in my attempts at a new and improved life. I planned to take a full load this semester and vowed I'd strive for a 4.0 in every class.

I did, however, begin to see why they offered 'goof off" classes in college, since I felt I was burning myself out. I opted to do something different by finally learning to play guitar. The music department, as you'd expect, had instructors who teach musical instruments. You don't need to know how to play before getting to college. So, as a minor escape from all the academic courses, I also took *Guitar 101*. It was difficult at first, due to throbbing fingers, until I built up calluses. I found I enjoyed playing in the solitude of my home, and often used practice and 'plunking' as therapy, and for those nights I couldn't sleep. Also, much to my surprise, I began singing along with my playing.

Feeling distracted at times, I told myself I was just not man enough to hold Isabel Grey, who was definitely going places.

Though we'd promised to stay in contact via email, they were few and far between. About two months after she started at MIT, I received a long-awaited email. She opened with:

"Hi, how ya doin'? Hey, I wanted you to know I met this guy..."

I immediately hit the *Delete* key and erased the email. Feeling my guts twist, I didn't want to hear all the details. I never wrote back and deleted without reading all further emails from her. So, she had moved on, and my fears were realized. I'd have to move on also.

As Fred, I'd done well, but should have been more dedicated to pursuing some goal, rather than taking things as they came. I wished I'd invested in my marriage and family life as well as I had in my career and financial dealings. Somewhere, I'd read something about 'no success in business can compensate for failure in the home,' or something like that. As Fred, I was guilty of that very thing. Now, as Bill Hollister, I needed to excel to the best of my ability, in some endeavor I felt was worthwhile. My problem was I didn't have a clear vision of what that should be. I had set my priorities with degree first, then I could explore a relationship with a marriage and family, so I could then improve on that aspect of my former life. With that in mind, I tried to keep a low social profile, lest I get distracted again. Sometimes it was difficult to shut oneself off completely.

I ran into Rachel now and again, since she was doing post-grad work, and she finally took the initiative and asked me to take her to dinner. Feeling odd, since she was Isabel's friend, I was sure Izzy would hear about it. Taking her to a nice restaurant, I tried to show her a good time, but I was on my best behavior. As I was driving her back to the campus, she finally asked:

"Come on, Bill! I know you're afraid to make any advances because Isabel could find out! You never told her so, but I think you love her, a lot. She could've gone to a much closer college, but she wasn't sure how you felt. She told me you were giving her space because you're sure she'll find someone else."

"She never told me she loved me, either," I hedged. "I assumed she was just making up for not having a boyfriend for two years. I knew she'd move on from me to something better! I just didn't want her to feel she couldn't be free to date at MIT. Yes, I love her, but I was afraid to tell her because she has her whole life ahead of her, and I didn't want to restrict her in any way!"

"For such a smart guy, you're pretty stupid! If you'd told her you loved her, she'd probably have stayed here for her Masters. UTA has a pretty good engineering school! Not as prestigious as MIT, but not bad!" Rachel raved.

"That's exactly why I said nothing! I want her to be all she can be, and she doesn't need me to hold her back from getting her degree from a place like MIT. I would always feel guilty. Besides, I'm sure she's moved on by now," I fumed.

"You're such a sad, sad man! Since you're sure she'll find someone there, I think we both need you to take me to your place, and we'll bang the hell out of each other ! There won't be any strings, and I promise I won't tell Iz. She asked me to keep an eye on you, but she didn't tell me to lay you! That's my own idea! The truth is: I need it!" Rachel confided.

"Rachel, the offer is tempting. I'm not sure how I'll do, but I've always had the fantasy of hooking up with the whole Gaggle," I admitted.

"Isabel always raved about how great you were in bed, so I want to know if she was just bragging, or if you're really a stud! And two out of five isn't bad!" she said enthusiastically.

In the end, I took Rachel home and we spent the night together. Yes, I felt guilty in my mind and in my heart, but I rationalized it by reminding myself Isabel had moved on. The next morning, as I was taking her back to the dorm, Rachel offered to give testimonials. We laughed about it, and she was just being kind, I'm sure. Rachel was pretty good, but she wasn't Isabel!

By semester's end, my efforts paid off well. I earned 4.0s in all my courses, including *Guitar 101*. My finals week was very busy, and I took Rachel out afterwards, to celebrate our successful completion of another semester. Rachel was working on her Masters, of course, so her work never really stopped. During the semester, Rachel and I got together every couple weeks so we could take out our sexual frustrations on each other. No emotional attachment ever developed, at least not on my part, but we became close friends.

Hilary returned a couple times to visit her junior boyfriend, but by her second visit, he'd moved on, so she found herself at loose ends. Rachel suggested I show Hilary what she'd missed the time I'd refused her. I began feeling like a gigolo, but Hilary was very effusive in her praise and also vowed never to tell Isabel. That made me feel even more guilty, but I told myself to face the fact Isabel had moved on by now. So, why shouldn't I? I realized I needed to take stock of my progress.

As soon as the semester ended, I took a short road trip to see Drs. Randquist and Sweeney. While I was driving up to Kansas, I had a lot of time to think. I reviewed all I'd accomplished since I was 'renewed.' In comparison, I was carrying on with the great start the previous tenant in my body had started, education-wise, and vowed I'd complete my degree, and go even further. As Fred Lambson, I'd married young, not out of love, really. I met my wife socially, and everyone said we made a good couple, so we got married. Not a good reason, in retrospect. My relationship with my wife had never been cultivated. She stayed home and took care of the children, while I earned the living. We kept our roles separate, and pursued our own interests, so it was no wonder our relationship fell apart after the children left home. We'd never created an 'us' relationship. As I began as Bill Hollister, I vowed not to consider marrying right away, as I felt I'd be falling right back into the same rut!

Chastising myself for getting involved with Isabel so soon into my new life, I re-dedicated myself to remain aloof and unfettered. I was determined to pursue success in a manner different from my former life. In a moment of clarity, however, I had to admit the heart was not as logical as the brain and holds no allegiance to it. A heart can be lost at the most inopportune time! I'd given my heart to Isabel, but she never knew it! So, things turning out the way they did made it one less thing to worry about! I'd just have to be more circumspect in my personal life from this point on, so I could succeed, and not get bogged down with relationships! I would make that my new mantra.

I spent the last few miles before getting home gathering my thoughts, about what I figured the doctors would be concerned with. Since I'd given them prior notice of my arrival, they were prepared for me. They conducted several mental acuity and physical coordination tests and asked a whole passel of questions. Dr. Randquist had a private counseling session with me, and we discussed nearly every-thing I'd thought about since I came into Bill Hollister. Telling him about Isabel, I related to him how I felt during our relationship, and announced it was over. Not being a psychol-ogist, he never commented, except to ask me how I felt about it. I admitted I loved her, but also hedged by saying the breakup was for the best. He pursed his lips but said nothing. Near the end of our session, I brought up the reflexive response I felt during the fight I had on campus. He had no answers but took it down in his notes. He did remark that it could have been a form of 'muscle memory' but didn't go any further.

The drive back to UTA seemed longer, as I felt near physical pain from missing Isabel. I had thought to exorcise her from my heart by talking to Dr. Randquist, but I think it just testified to me how I really felt about her, and it hurt more to realize I'd given her up so easily. Once back in Austin, the rest of the break I hardly left home except to run and spent all my time with my music. Knowing I'd never be a Tony Mottola or Richard Smith, I wasn't planning on performing anyway, so I just enjoyed practicing and playing. During the last semester, I'd been required to give a recital, with all the other students, and had chosen a ballad from my 'other' life: an old Kingston Trio song from the sixties called "Scotch and Soda." It had a fine guitar backing, and the words were minimal. My instructor was familiar with the song, so judged it on its merits. The audience didn't get the song, but my delivery was appreciated.

When my last semester began, I buckled down to give nearly one hundred percent of my efforts to my studies. I only took time to visit the range occasionally, for practice and the club, with all new members, who held their own at meets. By then, I was sure I would stay at UTA for my Masters. I was already a TA for a couple math professors and had taught a dozen class sessions in addition to helping them administer and grade exams. Professor Taggert had even contacted me to be a guest speaker in one of his history classes. I was surprised, since history was only my minor, but I think I enjoyed giving that lecture as much if not more than I did my math lectures. Because of the response he had from students, he requested I return, and I ended up doing it twice more. So, between being a math TA, and the occasional history lecturer, I was beginning to think about being a teacher after all!

As I began my opening remarks for my last presentation of the semester in Math 7, I looked into the lecture hall gallery and recognized five familiar faces half-way up the tiered rows.

The Gaggle, re-assembled for the first time in almost a year, was sitting together. All of them! Isabel sat in the middle. To her right sat Laurette and Cyndee. Cyndee was obviously pregnant. Rachel and Hilary were on her left. Everyone looked much the same, except for Cyndee's baby bulge. I lost my train of thought for a second; causing me to hem and haw a few times before I recovered. My mind was in turmoil, but the material was familiar, and I slipped into 'autopilot.' After presenting my lecture, I asked some questions and fielded a few from the audience. Then it was over, and I was packing my backpack preparatory to going out the side door like usual.

Suddenly, I was surrounded by five attractive women. There was a group hug and a few kisses on my cheeks. Looking around, I felt a little embarrassed. Rachel I was used to seeing, but I had put the others out of my mind, feeling I would never see any of them again. All of them were speaking at once, bringing me up to date on what they were doing.

Hilary had a job, with no plans to continue her education. Cyndee was married to a dentist and was helping in his office until the baby was due. Laurette was attending Texas A&M in College Station, Texas, working on her Masters. Isabel was silent, letting the others run out of news. I felt her eyes on me.

Rachel spoke up: "As I told all of you: Bill's been a busy man! He probably teaches more classes than the profs he's working for. He's even good at it! Have you decided where you'll go for your Masters yet?"

"Uh, most likely be here. I guess I'm too lazy to change schools!"

"You look good on that dais! You should become a professor, and to hell with private industry!" This from Cyndee.

"I'm thinking more and more about it. I never thought I'd want to be a teacher, but it's been very fulfilling."

Laurette began talking to Rachel, and Hilary was in discussion with Cyndee about married life. This left Isabel and me just standing there. Looking at her, she finally brought her eyes to mine.

"So... how's life in New England?" I opened.

"It's okay, but the seasons are really different there. It was a bad winter. I couldn't seem to stay warm," Isabel answered.

"What's wrong with your boyfriend? Wasn't he doing his job?" I quipped.

"What boyfriend?" she asked.

"You know: the one you were telling me about, in the last email I read, before I stopped writing," I countered.

Seeming to go into a trance, Isabel paused for about a half a minute, then her eyes opened wide, and she took a deep breath. "You didn't read the entire email, did you?"

"I'm sorry Izzy, but when you said you'd met this guy... it just hurt too much to go on. I couldn't bear reading how you felt about him and all the painful details."

She smiled tightly but looked at me as though trying to make up her mind about something. Finally, she asked suddenly, "Do you love me?"

Caught off guard, I answered without thought. "Yes, I do, but what difference does it make? You've got a boyfriend!" I sputtered.

"For someone getting ready to graduate, you are such a poor, miserable idiot! I'm really pissed with you, Bill!"

"I've never claimed to be smart! Educated, yes! Smart, no!" I said, defensively.

"If you'd bothered to read the *whole* email, you'd have learned I'd met this guy... from your hometown, and he had so many expressions and mannerisms like yours, I was amazed you and he weren't related. His name was Eric Lambson"—my/Fred's oldest grandson!—"I asked him if he knew you, and he said the name was familiar, but couldn't place it! I was assigned to a study group he was in, and we struck up a conversation one evening. The group broke up after a week or so, and I just saw him in the lecture hall, but we never spoke again. I just thought it was funny and wanted to tell you! Is that why you never wrote back to me? Because you thought I had a boyfriend? Oh, Bill! I want to scream! I've been in agony, thinking you were with someone else, and had no feelings for me anymore. I've missed you so much and couldn't get you out of my mind. I couldn't wait for the semester to end, so I could come back here and find out what was going on! Rachel told me you weren't with anyone, and I wanted to believe her, but when you stopped writing, I just *knew* you had someone else!"

"Isabel, there hasn't been anyone but you! I've hurt ever since you left." Rushing into my arms, she crushed herself against me, sobbing. "Don't cry, Izzy. I love you so very much!"

Pulling her head from my chest, she looked up. "I love you too, Bill! I've missed being in your arms."

Bending to kiss her upturned lips, I felt hers quivering with emotion. We were totally alone in our minds, so the kiss was desperately passionate. From behind us, we heard:

"Awww, ain't they sweet? We might as well go, girls. I think these two want to be alone, somewhere else!" Rachel remarked.

"Ah *hem*! Get a room, you two!" kibitzed Hilary.

Breaking our kiss, we looked at the others and grinned sheepishly. The lecture hall was empty, so we prepared to leave.

"What do you ladies have planned?" Isabel asked.

"We thought we'd see who's taken over our table. Rachel says a new group claimed it. We just wanted to see if they're up to our standards!" said Cyndee. Isabel replied:

"We think we'll pass. Can we all get together at your place, Bill? Later, that is!"

"Sure. How about seven this evening. I can cook if you'd like."

Rachel looked at the others, and then said: "We'll pick up something to prepare. You'll need to keep up your strength, lover boy!"

By the time the others arrived at my place, Isabel and I had ironed out all the wrinkles in our relationship and were temporarily sated. Fresh out of the shower, she had to put her same clothes on, since her clean clothes were in her car, still on campus. Ordinarily, my spirit would have soared, but my conscience had a hefty anchor holding me down.

Reading my mood, Isabel quietly asked: "You need to get something off your chest?"

"I didn't think I'd ever see you again, and I'm a healthy male, and..." I attempted.

"And she was so willing!" Isabel finished.

"Who?" I asked quizzically.

"Whoever!" Isabel retorted.

"Yes, but it was only physical! She could never replace you in my heart! I'm sorry, I really am!" I whined.

"I know! I told her to keep an eye on you! I didn't tell her to keep up your morale."

"Who?" I blurted.

"Rachel, of course!" Isabel volunteered.

"You knew?" I asked, incredulously.

"Men aren't the only ones with a conscience. Hilary has one too!" Isabel said sagely.

"Oh, Izzy. I'm so sorry!" I pleaded.

"You were lifting *her* morale, after her boy-toy dumped her. Anyone else?"

"No! I swear!" I pledged.

"Only because Laurette and Cyndee weren't here! I know about your fantasy," Isabel smirked.

"Then why don't you hate me? I betrayed you with two of your friends and have lusted after the other two! I won't blame you if you do," I said penitently.

"All that's in the past—or better be! It also bears out my belief you have good taste! You kept it within The Gaggle," Isabel said smartly.

"You're a strange woman, Isabel Grey! One of a kind, and I don't want to ever let you go!" I said wonderingly.

"Could I get that in writing?" she asked.

"Okay, do you want that typewritten, or handwritten, in blood?" I inquired.

"No, and don't get nervous, but I'd really prefer it on a marriage license!"

"I'll see what I can do! When are you going back to MIT?" I asked.

"Never!" she blurted.

"Never? Why not?" I shouted.

"Because I can get my Master's here, just as easy; because MIT is full of haughty geeks; and because my preferred study partner is here!" She kissed me, softly at first, then with increasing passion.

"Aren't you guys finished yet?" Rachel said, as she banged through the door, arms full of grocery sacks. The other three were right behind, so Isabel and I got up and began organizing the preparation of the meal.

During the meal, Izzy asked: "What's this I hear about you taking up folk singing?"

"I'm not a folksinger," I scoffed.

"Well, country singer, then?" she said, correcting herself.

"I, madam, am a balladeer!" I bragged.

"Whatever! How come you never sang to me?" she inquired.

"I just learned how to play guitar last semester and began singing along, just for something to do!" I answered.

"When dinner is over, we want to be entertained! Don't we, girls?" Isabel said.

Rachel was enthusiastic since she'd heard me play and

sing. The others weren't quite so adamant. Isabel would not relent, so after the dishes were cleared up, we adjourned to the living room, and I gave a command performance, reprising my recital piece and following up with songs most of them had never heard of: "Danny's Song," "Embraceable You," "Stardust," and "She's Always a Woman." After five songs, I stopped. Nearly everyone clamored for more, but I knew I'd better stop before things got tedious. Most all The Gaggle had positive comments, but some were merely being polite, I was sure. Isabel made me promise to give her a private show, which elicited a few catcalls.

During a lull, Isabel remarked: "Does anyone want to help me plan a wedding?"

Four pairs of eyes grew large, and then the squeals began. I immediately became a superfluous member of the party. But the evening ended with the girls in a giddy mood. Rachel gave Isabel a ride back on campus to pick up her car, while I quickly cleaned the bathroom and changed the linen for my house-guest.

If you're following closely, you know I never actually proposed, except to say I never wanted to let her go, but it was apparently close enough for both of us. On graduation day, I got my diploma, and instead of going to a graduation party, I went to the church on campus and was married to Isabel. Cyndee was the Matron of Honor, and the other three members of The Gaggle were bridesmaids. I didn't know who to ask to be Best Man, so I asked Professor Ernst. He'd been my mentor in my efforts to earn my BS, so I was closer to him than anyone else. We had a full month before I started my quest for my Masters! Isabel applied to transfer her course work for her Masters from MIT, and continue it at UTA.

I surprised her and took her to Hawaii for our honeymoon. I knew my nest egg wouldn't last forever, but this was a special occasion. When I got back, I'd have to look around for a job to supplement my dwindling account. In the meantime, Isabel and I acted just like you'd expect a honeymooning newlywed couple to act. We didn't go out many days before noon, but we managed to get respectable tans. Man, did she look good in the half-dozen bikinis I bought her!

Chapter 13

Returning to Austin, I immediately started searching for a part time job. Isabel felt she should also. For me, I was fortunate enough to find an evening job, teaching math at an adult education center. They were willing to accept my BS degree and my TA teaching experience. They were looking for range masters at our local firing range, and though it wasn't making use of her degree, Isabel had flexible hours and could do a bit of studying on the side. Our schedules didn't allow us much time together, but we usually had the weekends.

Since Bill Hollister had declared in the beginning that he was going for his Masters, I still had entitlements on the G.I. Bill, but it was almost used up. Our course load was lighter, now we were post-graduates, but the study and research time increased. A very important part of a successful thesis was selecting the right topic. I was fortunate to have Professor Ernst as my thesis supervisor. He knew whether it had been attempted before. He gave me some ideas, and I mulled it over for a few days before registering my topic. The written abstract wasn't so difficult. My writing skills had always been good, even when I was *someone else*. Once my topic was registered, I went into research mode full tilt. Isabel had already declared her topic while at MIT and continued her research in that vein.

There were nights as we sat poring over research material that we would not speak but occasionally reach out and caress the other. This usually resulted in making eye contact momentarily, evoking a smile and perhaps an 'air kiss.' Though we were working on completely different projects, we could feel the emotional support of the other, and it added immensely to our mental wellbeing. Both of us had our own laptop computer, but we shared a printer, which was no inconvenience. When the writing phase for the thesis began, we spent long hours writing until one of us would stretch and do something to get the attention of the other. If both were amenable, we'd get up and go, just to get away and relieve some of the stress of the project. Isabel began running with me, making it more enjoyable. We'd also do silly things like miniature golf, or see a movie, or just go to the park and walk for an hour or so. And, at Izzy's urging, I serenaded her occasionally, to keep up my playing and singing skills! It all ended up as great tension relief. Although sex was good for that too, we kept lovemaking as something extra special and gloried in the mutual pleasure we shared.

If you disciplined yourself, you could earn a Masters in two and a half years, but there are those who tried to do it along with full time employment and sometimes a family. Isabel and I decided we wanted to get it over with, so we were driven, and finished the coursework earlier than most. Of course, since Isabel had started before me, she finished before me, and turned her thesis in, while I continued my research and writing. While she waited for her review and publishing, she worked full-time at the firing range, and when she was home, she assisted me in any way she could. When I finally finished and turned my thesis in, we took a couple days and went to San Antonio, where we took in tourist sights such as The Alamo and the Riverwalk. After that, it was just a waiting game, and we both continued working: Izzy at the range and me at Adult Ed—biding our time, and adding to our bank account. The time it took to earn our Masters had seemed to fly by, in retrospect, but the waiting became tedious.

Finally, the day arrived, and we were each awarded our

degree. I was now in the market for a job, though I could have continued immediately toward my PhD and try for a professorship. Isabel had applied for employment at several technology-based firms. Now she had her Master's degree in hand, the offers started coming in. Since we knew we'd be leaving Austin, we tried to get The Gaggle together for a reunion. Cyndee was taking care of her young son, Rachel and Laurette had their Masters in hand and had relocated to opposite ends of the country. Hilary was in Houston working, so she traveled to Austin one weekend, and we had a small party with Hilary and Cyndee, who left her son with her husband. It was a slightly sad gathering without the entire group and the fact it would be further splintered by Isabel's leaving for someplace yet to be determined. Promises were made, however, to keep in touch.

Isabel traveled for interviews at several companies based in diverse places across the country, but the best position she was offered was in St. Louis. I'd been to St. Louis a few times as Fred Lambson, and I knew the city, though I'd never been enchanted by the place. Now I had to change my perspective, as this would be where my soulmate would be employed. I immediately did a search of institutions of higher learning. Coming up with several possibilities, I sent my resume and cover letter to each of them right away. Believing I would find something, we packed our meager belongings in a small U-Haul and hitched it behind my Subaru.

Since my old home was on my way, we stopped off so I could see my doctors. Isabel knew I was getting a re-check for the lightning strike. During the counseling with Dr. Randquist, we had a long discussion.

"Well, Bill, are you happy so far with your 'do over'?" he asked.

"I don't think I could be happier. I still have things to do, but I've earned not just one degree, but two. I've found a woman I can't imagine being without," I gushed. I had introduced him to Isabel, so he knew her somewhat.

"Well, I see one reason for your happiness. She seems like quite the woman. I foresaw your marriage because of the feelings you revealed during our last session, even with your disclaimers to the contrary. I'm also pleased to hear about your academic success. I knew you were driven to succeed, but I didn't want to dampen your spirit by cautioning you not to drive yourself to the point of hating yourself if you *didn't* succeed. And now, you want to be a teacher of mathematics. That's quite amazing, Bill. I'm hopeful this will be a fulfilling endeavor for you, and perhaps you'll find solace at last, and put aside your former regrets. You are really just beginning, and you have many more years to work toward finally being satisfied with your second chance," he advised.

"Thank you, doc. I am still amazed at my good fortune not to have to go to my grave with regrets. I'm sure many people do. I was just at the right place, at the right time, with the right doctors. I'm very grateful to you and Dr. Sweeney," I exclaimed.

"Dr. Sweeney and I just did the little bit of technology required to give you a new life. You, Bill, did all the hard work, with rehabilitation, and starting off on your quest, which was no mean feat. So, you're quite welcome, Bill. Is there anything else you wanted to add? Any new manifestations or occurrences we should be aware of?" he questioned.

"No. I don't think so. Out of curiosity, have you had any other chances to repeat your experiment?" I queried.

"We've had a couple chances, but not to the extent nor success we had with you. We keep our eyes and ears open for another opportunity. Please stay in touch. I'm glad you'll be in St. Louis, as it's closer to us. Good luck, Bill, and maybe you could be more forthcoming with your progress. Two visits in three years isn't as we'd expected. Just an email would be helpful, and we could also update you on any new experiments. Of course, it's still confidential. Hope to be in contact soon. Best wishes for you and your wife." He said as he ushered me out of his office, and into the waiting room, where he knew Isabel was waiting, reading a magazine. He bid us both farewell.

"So, how did the counseling session go?" Isabel asked me, as we left the hospital.

"It went well, and the doctors are pleased with my progress: from a *brain-dead hulk* to a future mathematics teacher!" I jokingly commented.

She was not amused and gave me a pitiful, withering look. Pretending not to notice, I put her in the car, and we continued to St. Louis.

Chapter 14

When Isabel accepted the position at her new company, she was told the company would put us up at an extended stay hotel to give us a chance to find a place to live. The apartment choices weren't great close to her work, which was in midtown, so we had to search farther out of the city. We finally found a place in University City. It required a lease, and the rent was steep, but with both Isabel's income and mine, when I found a job, we felt we could afford it. Public transportation was well established, so we both planned to use it to commute to work, saving wear and tear on our trusty Subaru, which was now five years old.

When Isabel reported for work at her new employer, they moved her around at first, trying to see where she fit in. It didn't take them long to realize her potential. She was such a livewire; she seemed to grasp research concepts readily and always had new ideas. She seemed destined for success, and for this reason, her management put her on a fast track to promotion. That's my girl! One of the aspects of her job was frequent travel. She seemed to take it in stride, and though it was tough on me, sitting home alone, it was the nature of the beast.

While Isabel was dazzling her bosses, I attempted to find out what all my letter writing efforts had wrought. Since I'd been on the move, it took a while for my rejection letters to catch up to me, and I even visited some of the places I had written to and was told I should have received their letter telling me they had no position available. Eventually, I was offered a probationary position at Fontbonne University, as an Adjunct Professor of Mathematics. The job was contractual and could be voided very easily. It also meant I got the leavings from the tenured professors. Though I had the requisite Master's degree, my lack of experience in front of the class was to my detriment until I revealed my experience at Adult Ed, and my saving grace was my time as a TA at UTA. The university called Professor Ernst to verify my claim, and he gave a glowing report. Within a few months, I felt the need to work toward my PhD, since it was apparent I would not go far in this field without a doctorate. This was what I wanted, right? To succeed the second time around! I knew I was pushing myself by striving to outdo my previous *self*.

In talking it over with Izzy, she felt she should start her PhD soon, but not right away, as she was still finding her depth. Eventually, she would need her doctorate, to be in line for further steps up the ladder. At present, she was working very hard to find her niche. Part of this was the constant travel. It was usually with a team, where they would visit with clients and contractors presenting the product lines the company was developing. It seemed she was gone all the time, and although I was busy getting up to speed as a professor, I still felt the loss of companionship when she was gone.

"So, how long will this trip be?" I asked Isabel, as I helped her pack.

"We should be back by Friday evening. Carl, Chuck, and Shelby will be there with me, and we're going to show them our new control panel, hoping we can get them to manufacture it for us. They've a good track record, and the company has used them before for smaller assemblies. We'll be meeting with their upper management and then their engineers. Carl and Shelby have the lead on this, so I'm there to observe and learn how they do things the company way," she explained.

"Oh, yeah, I remember meeting them all at the *get-acquainted* social, a couple weeks ago," I admitted.

"That's right. You have met them. Anyway, I'm sure I'll learn a lot, and someday, I hope to have the lead on a trip. I know I can handle it," she exclaimed.

"Yes, Iz, I know you can do *anything* you set your mind to," I told her, encouragingly.

"Thanks, lover. I know you support me," she told me as she caressed my face. "Would you like to take advantage of me one more time, before I have to dress?" Isabel said with a smoky look in her eyes.

"I never want to take advantage of you, but I *would* enjoy access to your sweet self before you go," I murmured, taking her into my arms. An hour later, I took her luggage to the cab and kissed her before she left for the airport. It would be a long four days, I thought wistfully.

Thursday evening, on a whim, I decided to call Isabel to see how things were going and to hear her voice. As late as it was, she should've been in her room. Dialing her number, I waited through three rings, then...

"Hello?" answered a man's voice.

Glancing at my phone to verify the dialed number, I did mental shrug and replied, "Sorry. I must have dialed the wrong number." I then broke the connection.

I was confused and looked again at the phone to see the number I'd dialed. It was Isabel's number. What just happened? I was inclined to call back and demand to know what was going on, but I was afraid to find out. I sat there with a sick, heavy feeling in the pit of my stomach. My mind kept lurching around with plausible explanations. I slept fitfully all night, and dragged myself to the university the next day, Friday. I finished for the week and was sitting apprehensively at home when Isabel came through the door, struggling with her bags. I automatically rushed to help her with her luggage, taking it into the bedroom.

Thanking me and giving me a kiss on the cheek, she sighed and slumped onto the bed.

"How did it go?" I asked stoically.

"We had a good trip. I think they'll accept the job, and I think we'll have to go back a couple more times to get all the kinks out of their manufacturing process," she said enthusiastically.

"That's good. It *must* have been a good trip!" I said with rancor.

"What does *that* mean? What's up, Bill?" she asked.

"What were you doing last night?" I questioned.

"I was working, Bill! What do you think I was doing?"

"I have no idea, but when I called you, a man answered your phone," I shouted.

"What? I was alone in my room, Bill. Don't you trust me?" she asked.

"It just makes me wonder what you were doing at MIT while you were there. I bet you weren't celibate," I accused.

"As a matter of fact, I *was* celibate. I was missing *you*, you jerk! And what were *you* doing in Austin? You were screwing my friends!" she retorted and began crying.

"So, who was it? Carl or Chuck?" I barked.

"It was neither! I wasn't with *anyone*," she sobbed.

"Then who answered your phone?" I rephrased.

"Are you sure you called my number?" Isabel muttered.

"Yes. I made certain," I jeered.

"When did you call?" she said tearily.

"About seven-thirty, your time there," I answered.

"I wasn't even in my room then. We were still at dinner, doing a review of the visit." she protested.

"So, where was your phone?" I mused.

"I kept it by me, to refer to notes. Wait! I had to go to the restroom and left my phone on our table! You must have called while I was gone, and one of the guys picked it up," she sputtered. "I would never cheat on you, Bill. I love you too much, and I thought you trusted me," she added.

Suddenly, I was agonized. "Oh, Izzy! I'm so, so, sorry!" I cried.

"Yes! You *are* sorry. You are one sorry individual to think I would step out on you," she accused.

"I guess I'm still not sure I'm man enough for you, Isabel. You're meant for great things, and as you say: I'm a sorry individual," I mumbled.

"Damn it, Bill. Stop putting yourself down! I love you and could give a crap about anything, or anybody, as long as I can be with you. I don't care if we live in a shack and eat beans and tortillas."

"I'm very sorry, Isabel. I just can't fathom what you see in me. You deserve much better. You deserve someone who won't be jealous and accuse you of things when you're totally innocent. I do love you and promise to trust you," I vowed.

"Well, we'll see. Right now, I'm hurt and sad and just need my man to cuddle with me. Sex is out tonight! I just want to be comforted. Okay?" she sniffed.

"Anything you want, Isabel. I'll try much harder to prove I'm worthy," I groveled.

"Knock off the *pity party*! You're worthy!" she snapped.

"Yes, ma'am!" I mumbled.

And that was our first major argument. From then on, she would call me each evening she was away traveling, and we'd murmur *sweet nothings* to each other over the phone.

Chapter 15

We were each dedicated to our jobs, but it didn't change the fact we were dedicated to each other more. I was determined to make a better life for me and my wife, not repeating the mistakes I had made the first time around. My quest for my doctorate was secondary to our devotion to each other. During my first semester break, Isabel was able to take a couple days off, and we drove down to Branson, Missouri, just to say we'd been there. Still very much in love, we had no time for anyone else. Oh, we had a small circle of friends, either from the university or her company, but they were casual friends and we spent less than one night a week with them.

During our trip, both on the road and while we weren't seeing the sights, we found ourselves in discussion. This was not new, since our conversations were quite eclectic, and we talked about everything under the sun. But the two major topics were Isabel's parents and our possible future children. I'd never met her parents, though she'd talked about them often. They lived in Florida now, and she maintained contact with them via bi-monthly phone calls. She'd last visited them on her way to MIT, and now they were asking to see her again.

"My mom and dad are wondering when they'll get to meet the man who stole me away from them," she opened.

"If they think I stole you from them, I'm dead already," I sighed.

"They were angry they weren't invited to our wedding. As an only child, they expected to be involved. I put off explaining why they weren't because I didn't have a good excuse. I was caught up in getting you under my control, I totally spaced on everything else," she chortled slyly.

"Well, not to start you yelling at me again, but I'd say you didn't want to let them see the sorry guy you were marrying. You were ashamed of me!" I jokingly ventured. That elicited a sharp slap to my arm, but not hard enough to make me lose control of the car.

"Stop that! I'll never be sorry I captured you. If I hadn't grabbed you the first day you stepped on campus, there'd been so much competition, I would've lost out," she exclaimed.

"I hardly think so. I never saw another woman on campus who could compete. As Tim Latham told me that first day: you were the *Queen Babe!*"

"Tim said that about me? Why, the sweet little imp! But getting back to my parents: they want to know when they're going to meet you," Isabel questioned.

"Are they wanting us to come down there, or them to come to St. Louis?" I inquired.

"We've no room, and they don't either. No matter where, a hotel or motel will be involved," she advised.

"If we go to Florida, it will have to be during a semester break. If they come to St. Louis, it would still be better during a break. Of course, it will also require you taking time off, unless you're going to stick me with entertaining them while you're at work. In that case, you may come home and find me *drawn and quartered*! Or even worse: neutered!" I complained.

"Hah! They don't think *that* badly of you," she defended.

"Well, a guy can't be too sure about doting parents," I grumbled.

The second topic was *children*. It had been mentioned before, in passing, and was something we assumed would eventually bubble to the top of our priority list. I was always careful not to act like an authority on *children: the joys and heartaches of having them.* I did, however, tell her how smart and beautiful I thought her children would be. She was now twenty-eight, and I was thirty. She told me she thought she was ready to try.

"I'm glad you said that, because we've been *practicing* for a while, and now can add *trying* to have children, which is just as much fun!" I leered. That got me a sly look and a trip back to the motel room.

She told me, after we'd finished: "I'll bet you can't wait to make my flat tummy bulge all out of shape, can you?"

"As the saying goes: Don't take seriously what I poke in jest!" I smirked. Oh, that wonderful, tinkly laugh. It made me want to take her back to bed. We'd have to wait longer for the *trying* part, since Isabel still had her IUD. She assured me she'd schedule a doctor's appointment after the removal to make sure everything was working normally, and the *advanced fun* would begin!

Upon her return to work, and during a casual conversation with Shelby, Isabel mentioned in passing how she and I were interested in starting our family. It didn't take long for the information to get back to Isabel's supervisor, Henry Wease.

During their next private conversation, he inquired: "Isabel, er, I mean, Mrs. Hollister, I understand you and your husband are planning to have a baby."

Knowing the source of his information, she simply said: "We've discussed it. Is there a problem?"

"Uh, no, no. I, uh, we can't dictate to you how you conduct your personal life. However, you've demonstrated your superb ability to excel within the company, and we've confidence in your taking on greater responsibility for rapid advancement. I, uh *we* feel your decision to start a family could possibly sideline or derail your progress. Please review your decision carefully to determine if it's wise at this moment in time. You're still young," he pontificated.

"Mr. Wease, I'm a dedicated engineer and scientist, but I'm also a woman. I'm approaching the upper limit of my child-bearing years. I did not pursue this career just to throw it away because I decided I *needed* a kid. My husband and I would like to create something, between us, that is worthwhile and wonderful. I assure you, if we're successful in having a child, barring any unforeseen medical reasons, I plan on being fully productive and employed up to the last possible minute before the birth of our child and expect to return to full employment as quickly as is medically wise. You will not be disappointed, sir!" she spouted.

"Uh, thank you, Isabel. I believe you've made your point. Please keep me informed as to your, uh, condition, and any short-range plans affecting the company. I apologize," he gulped.

"Thank you, Henry!" she exclaimed.

While continuing to dazzle her superiors with her brilliance, within two months of her IUD removal, we saw the positive indications on a home pregnancy test. I was quick to notify Drs. Randquist and Sweeney of the additional milestone, and they were quick to respond with congratulations. Isabel, in turn, notified her parents and the rest of The Gaggle.

As proud as I was of her, I knew this lent a new level of stress for Isabel. She'd started her career as a bright star, making herself known as the *go to* person, who quickly gained added responsibilities. Grooming her for greater things also made greater demands on her time, which made her adamant as to how many hours she felt she owed the company and how much travel she could tolerate, given her developing gravidity. The company was astute enough to realize the potential value she could bring them, so they were tolerant and patient. They immediately assigned someone to shadow her so they could bridge the gap while she was out on maternity leave.

In reflection, I was amazed at the contrast between my two

wives. Fred had married in a different era; a time when husbands earned the living and wives were the mothers, or at least homemakers. Feeling chauvinistic now, I wondered if my first wife had any ambitions outside the home. I never inquired! Even in that, Fred had failed to allow his wife to be all she could be. He'd taken for granted she'd be content to stay at home and keep it in order—for him! She had a social life, with women's groups and such, and I wondered what topics of conversation they had:

"I tell you; I know I could learn to do the stuff my husband does, and maybe better. If I could get out of the house, like he does, I'd be successful too!" I imagined some of them saying. I was much chagrined, thinking I was *all that* back then. Isabel may not be more intelligent than Fred's wife, but who will ever know! I just knew I was proud of Isabel now and backed her all the way. If her success eclipsed my own, so be it!

Isabel didn't seem to be bothered with morning sickness, which was great for both of us. Her mood swings were a little more intense, but nothing we couldn't handle. As she began to show, I realized I'd forgotten how beautiful an expectant mother could be. Isabel was even more so. She was simply radiant and very tolerant of the mean old man who brought this curse upon her. She always managed to look so beautiful and had extremely good taste in her maternity wardrobe. Her superiors at work were overjoyed at the positive feedback they received from customers who dealt with her during her pregnancy. She dazzled them with her professional manner and stylish though gravid appearance.

One aspect of our impending happy event was me having to finally face up to her parents, who I'd yet to meet. So, I now had the opportunity to do so, since her mother wanted to be with Isabel when she delivered. Izzy wasn't so sure, since we'd been independent of others and made a good team on all other things in life. But her mother was very persuasive, and they flew to St. Louis when Isabel was within a week of her due date, just after the first of the new year. We met them at the airport and Isabel was just as nervous as I. I saw immediately where Isabel got some of her looks and her independence.

"Hi! Mom and Dad, I'd like you to meet my husband, Bill. Honey, this is my mom and dad: Lester and Vivian Grey," Isabel exclaimed. I shook hands with both parents, and they were cordial.

"So, the mystery man is finally revealed. We've wondered what kind of a man our Isabel would choose," Vivian intoned; her gaze told me she wasn't impressed.

"Glad to meet you, young man. I hope you're treating our daughter well," invoked Lester, or Les as he preferred.

"Mom, Dad, Bill treats me like a queen. Don't worry!" Isabel defended. They remained stiff and a bit stand-offish. Since we had a modest apartment, her parents stayed at the nearest hotel and came to our place each morning. Isabel was now on maternity leave of absence, but I had to keep teaching until she went into labor, and then I could take Family Medical Leave of Absence (FMLA). If I was not at the university, I felt like a piece of superfluous furniture. Isabel could see this and tried to get me involved with what she and her parents were doing. One evening, after they'd returned to their hotel:

"Oh, Bill, what's wrong? Are my parents so bad?" she inquired.

"They treat me like an old shoe. Half the time they don't even act like I'm here. It's like they look down their noses at me and think I'm not worthy of their daughter, which is what I've always maintained," I whined.

"Don't give me that *inferiority* crap!" Isabel snapped.

"I'm sorry! It's just you're their princess, and I probably seem like the court jester or village idiot," I snorted.

"Oh, poor baby! Don't worry, you're my king, and I'm your queen, and to hell with everyone else. But try to stay friendly with them, since they *are* my parents. They won't be here forever," she cajoled. It was frustrating for me, until she went into labor.

As Izzy's parents tolerated me, they were very much involved with our daughter as soon as she was born. Rebekkah Lyn Hollister came into the world at almost noon on a snowy January day in St. Louis, Missouri. She was a precious bundle, and we all adored her. Isabel was over the moon about our daughter, and I forced my way into her care, proving I was not inept with newborns. Due to my insistence about being involved in caring for Rebekkah, I forged a peace treaty between myself and her maternal grandparents. Before Les and Vivian left for home, they said to me, via Vivian:

"Bill, we're beginning to see what Isabel loves about you. We see the way you spoil her and your new daughter with love. You're certainly a mate worthy of our daughter, and we love you for it. Please take good care of both our girls!" I assured them I would.

When Isabel returned to work, she was able to take Rebekkah with her since her firm had a nursery and daycare on premises. It was a major perk that allowed Isabel to get back into the swing of things much quicker. It also allowed me to get back to the university. Our life together took on another dimension with our daughter's arrival, but we spent as much time as possible together, so I could bond with our daughter just like Isabel. Rebekkah was precocious and did everything ahead of the schedules in the baby books. It may have just been parental pride, but it was difficult not to treat her like a prodigy. We were determined to help her grow up as a confident, well-adjusted young woman who was outgoing and not stuck on herself. We realized our expectations were idealistic, and we expected other factors may creep in to affect and alter the shape of her psyche. We could only try our hardest and hope for the best. I don't remember discussing such things with my wife when I was Fred.

Chapter 16

Given the circumstances, I no longer had any contacts in the aerospace industry, but I kept my eye on how Isabel's company interfaced with other technology-based businesses. While doing my job as an adjunct professor of math, I also enrolled in some classes to help me on my quest for my PhD. It was done on a whim, but I thought it couldn't hurt me in my research. I was between semesters in teaching and was on a research errand to further the course work for one of my classes. While walking down the street, I happened to come face to face with Stephen, my—that is, Fred's—eldest son. It was a shock to me, but I'm pretty sure he didn't notice. He had no reason to recognize me, but I felt I should find some way to engage him in conversation.

"Pardon me, but could you direct me to the *Quick Reader* bookstore?" I asked.

"Sorry, but I'm just visiting and know very little about the city," he replied.

While we talked, I looked him over.

"Oh. Where are you from?" I enquired. He looked at me more closely, but the expression I wore was one of common interest. Glancing around, he saw nothing which set off any alarms in his mind, so he told me where he was from. Of course, I already knew that, but it gave me an opening gambit for continued conversation. He'd changed in the nearly four years since I'd seen him last. He was heavier, as was a genetic trait in Fred's family. He looked a little like I had, when I was

Fred, though he'd kept in better physical shape.

"Yes. I know that city. I attended college there for a while after being discharged from the military," I remarked.

"You look like someone I should know, but I don't recall. What's your name if you don't mind me asking?" he commented.

"My name is William Hollister. And yours?" I responded.

"I'm Stephen Lambson," he informed me.

"Uh, would you be related to Fredrick Lambson?" I continued.

"Yes. He was my father. Did you know him?" he returned.

"I never met him, but he gave me a grant while I was recovering from an accident. By the time I was well enough to thank him, I learned he'd passed away," I volunteered.

"Now I remember! Weren't you in a freak accident and in the same hospital where my father died? Uh, yes, you were struck by lightning or electrocuted or something. But they told me you were, uh, *brain dead*! Sorry to put it that way," he apologized.

"It's okay. They suspected I had irreversible brain damage, but here I am, a college professor! That might explain a lot about our institutions of higher learning, after all," I said, chuckling.

Stephen was taken aback by my humorous response to his forward comment. I assured him I took no offense, and we talked for a few moments longer. Then, I asked him if he had time to tell me a little about his father.

"Not much to say, really! He was successful, without having a degree, but he was adamant about his children getting an education, for which we're thankful. He and my mother eventually broke up, but it was amicable, so there was never a problem knowing they both cared about us. He lived his life pretty much how he wanted to and was over seventy when he passed. He may have lived longer, had he not done some things to excess. I'm not talking about tobacco or alcohol, but he loved his meat and desserts, and he lived a sedentary life with a lot of inherent stress. I really shouldn't be telling you all this. I've just never had anyone ask me about my dad before now," he muttered.

"I don't mean to pry, but I'm appreciative of your sharing that with me. If you don't mind me asking: Did you consider him a good father?" I inquired.

"Well, I guess you could say he was. He gave us all the material things we wanted, but he was strict at the same time, not letting us get out of hand, behavior wise. He didn't support us in our school and sports as much as our mother. He always told us he loved us but was never physical in showing it. I think I resented him a little, at the end, because he was still acting like he had the world by the tail. Yet, he was lying in that hospital bed, dying on us! I know he could've lived longer, if he'd taken better care of himself when he was younger. He tried to prepare us, though, so it wasn't as if he died suddenly, leaving us destitute. A lot of people get nothing when their parents die, but there was an inheritance for each of us. He was good about that, but what son or daughter is ever happy with what they get financially? I guess, looking back on it, I could have been a lot more grateful.

"I'm glad I talked to you, because you've made me realize my father wasn't as mean and cold as I've been thinking since he died. I only hope I do as well by my family as he did. I'm sorry, Mr., uh, Hollister, right? I'm sorry, but I must get to a business meeting. It was nice talking to you. Let me give you my business card, and if you want to call me another time, maybe we can talk again?" he ended.

"Sure, Mr. Lambson, I'd like to talk again. I'll give you a week or two before I bother you. I hope your business in St. Louis is successful. Thanks for telling me about your father. Good day," I responded.

As I watched my son walk away, I fought down the urge to go after him and have him accept that I was really his father reincarnated. I knew he'd think me demented and call the police. No one would believe me, and I had so much to lose by those actions. I had a new life, and I had been totally happy with it until just a few minutes ago. I had to contain myself and go about my errand as originally planned. It was difficult putting the chance encounter out of my mind. I'd received feedback on my life from my own son, and as biased as it may have been, I felt it was how he honestly felt about his deceased father. Although it was far from a validation of my first go-around in life, my ego wanted to sigh:

"I guess I wasn't so bad, after all!" Instead, I was determined even more to do better this time! I even thought, again, about if I should try to tell Isabel my true story. It could irrevocably affect our marriage, and above all, I wanted no part of anything that would hurt my beloved Isabel. If I were to lose her love, it would shatter me!

I continued my research for my doctorate along with teaching my college classes. I spent as much time as I could with Isabel and Rebekkah, wanting to give them the family life I had denied my first family. As Isabel continued to excel in every task assigned her, she felt it was time to begin pursuing her own doctorate, and her company told her they would support her efforts.

Amid everything going on in our life, we both shared responsibilities in caring for our daughter. At night, we'd take turns putting her to bed, while the other would use the spare time to work on our course work. One evening, I had just finished putting Rebekkah in her crib, where I usually sang her a soft melody *a capella*, and she seemed to enjoy my lullabies. Izzy was in the dining room on her computer. As I entered the room, I was about to say something, but I suddenly just blanked out.

"Bill? Bill, honey! What's wrong?" I heard Isabel pleading with me, as I became aware once more. She saw my eyes open and was more insistent. "Bill! Bill! Are you all right?" she shouted. I winced, so she spoke more softly. "Honey! What is it?" I realized she had my head cradled in her lap as she knelt on the floor.

"Uh, uh, I don't know what happened," I mumbled.

"You fell flat on your face, sweetie. I was afraid you'd break something. Are you all right?" She repeated.

"I, uh, think so. I was about to say something to you, and everything just went blank," I explained.

"Are you hurt anywhere? Can you get up?" She wept and tried to assist me in rising. Once on my feet, she steadied me and guided me to the sofa. I felt unsteady on my feet, my equilibrium a bit off. Once sitting, we discussed the event.

"Oh, Bill. You scared the hell out of me! What happened?" she quizzed.

"I don't know. I just blacked out! Maybe I'm overly tired, or maybe I'm hungry. I haven't eaten too much today," I supplied.

Uh, huh. And I bet you ran on the campus track between classes too! You've got to eat regularly, and you've been pushing yourself too hard. Oh, Bill, what am I going to do with you? Let me get you a drink and a snack," she fretted.

"I don't think I'm pushing myself any harder than you are. Besides, after running into *someone* I knew who reminded me how a friend had neglected himself and died prematurely, it just made me want to lead a healthier lifestyle," I argued.

"We don't eat that bad, and you get plenty of exercise. Much more than I."

"But you always look as beautiful as the day I first saw you, even after Rebekkah's birth," I admired.

"We're talking about you, my sweetheart. I just take after my mother. She still looks like she did in her twenties."

"And I'm the lucky guy who married her beautiful off-spring," I crowed.

"Stop! I'm worried about you, Bill. You need to go see a doctor. You haven't seen anyone besides your Drs. Randquist and Sweeney. I think you need to see someone local," she advised.

"I'm okay, now. Maybe I should just go to bed early. A good night's sleep should fix me right up," I bargained.

"Okay, but I'm keeping my eye on you. If anything else happens, I'll *carry* you to the doctor's if I have to. Got it?"

"Yes, ma'am!"

The next morning, I felt great and went to the university. I decided I wouldn't run and so studied instead. That night, everything went as usual and while Isabel took her turn putting our daughter to bed, I studied full tilt. After about an hour, I began getting a headache behind my eyes, and my neck hurt. Believing it was just stress, I took ibuprofen and went to bed at my normal time. The next day, I still had the headache and pain in my neck. I beat Isabel home but looked forward to my turn with Rebekkah. As I was in the middle of changing my clothes, things went blank once more. When I regained consciousness, I found myself on the floor, beside the bed. I lay there for a few minutes, allowing my faculties to recover, then I pulled myself up and onto the bed, where I continued to lie. After about ten minutes, I got up and continued dressing. I didn't tell Isabel about it when she got home, and I was able to fulfill my caring of our daughter. Afterwards, I decided I should email Dr. Randquist, since he knew more about my *condition* than anyone else. In the email, I told him about my blackouts, and about my head and neck aches.

The next day when I got home from work, I saw Dr Randquist had replied. "Bill, not to alarm you, but given your recent symptoms, I think it's imperative to either visit with me or a local physician as soon as possible. If what I suspect is happening, you could be in mortal danger. Please call me on my private line: ***-***-****, as soon as you can. Dr. Randquist," he wrote.

Since Isabel wasn't home yet, I made the call: "Hello, Dr Randquist. This is Bill Hollister."

"Bill, I'm glad you called. How are you feeling right now?" he asked.

"I still have a headache, and my neck hurts a little."

"That's not good. Could you come to the hospital tomorrow, as soon as possible? I don't want you flying. I really don't want you to drive, but if you can't get someone else to drive, we'll just have to chance it. Can you do that?" he inquired.

"I think so. I'll let my supervising professor know tonight. I'm not sure about Isabel's schedule, but if she can drive, we'll have to bring our daughter. What's wrong with me, doc?" I queried.

"I'm not sure, but I suspect you may have a brain aneurysm that could be leaking. But it could be several other maladies. We just need to ascertain whether that's the case. Try to relax, as stress could further your condition. Let me know as soon as possible when you'll be here. And, Bill, I'm glad you contacted me. I have a colleague who is a skilled neurosurgeon who deals with aneurysms regularly. Good luck, Bill, and keep me posted," he finalized.

As soon as Isabel came in the door, she saw the look on my face and asked: "What's wrong? Are you okay? Are my parents okay?"

"I didn't tell you about this, but I passed out again, yesterday in the bedroom, before you got home. I've also had a headache and neck ache the past couple days. I contacted Dr. Randquist, and I just got off the phone with him. He told me I may have a brain aneurysm, but he wants to make sure, and if I do, he wants them to operate there to take care of it. So, I have to get to his hospital as soon as I can," I confessed.

"We'll get you on a plane right away!" she offered.

"He doesn't want me on a plane. I did a little research while I waited for you, and the changes in cabin pressure could cause the vessel to break open. I need to drive there or have someone else drive me," I explained.

"You're not driving anywhere. I'll drive. It's about six hours, and we can leave tonight. I'll call Shelby and tell her, so she'll let my boss know. Is the Subaru up to it, or should I rent a car? I need to pack things for Rebekkah. If we rent, we'll have to change out the car seat," she barked. I smiled at her, and she gave me a questioning look.

"Oh, my beautiful Izzy! I see now why they've great plans for you. You immediately go into planning mode when presented with a problem. I love you, my sweet Isabel!" I gushed. She grinned at me, full of love.

"I love you, too, Bill. I don't want anything happening to my lover boy if I can help it! Now, how are we going?" she inquired.

"I think our trusty Subaru will get us there. I just had it serviced, and everything checked out. We'll gas up on our way out of town. Let's get Rebekkah packed, and then we'll pack a few things for us. If need be, we can get things we need while we're in town. I'll go online, and book us a hotel as close to the hospital as I can. Okay, sweetie, let's go!"

We were on the road in less than two hours. I called Dr. Randquist and gave him our estimated time of arrival. We packed a few finger foods for us to snack on, took extra formula for Rebekkah and a full diaper bag. Isabel was a competent driver and needed no navigator, so I tried to rest, though I didn't sleep deeply, my mind whirling with apprehension. Arriving at the hospital in the early hours of the morning, I was surprised to see Dr. Randquist and Dr. Sweeney there already.

"Well, Bill, we see you brought the family. As much as we

wanted to see your daughter, this is not the circumstances we wanted the meeting to take place. She is quite beautiful, and I can see you're both proud of her," Dr. Sweeney admitted.

"So, uh, may I call you Isabel?" Dr. Randquist requested.

"Yes, please. What's going to happen?" she insisted.

"We're going to put Bill through a series of tests. An MRI and an MRA, or angiography. This will see if he, in fact, has an aneurysm, and if he does, where it's located. If we detect one, we'll consult with our neurosurgeon colleague to get his opinion on its location, and a prognosis on its operability. It may take several hours. Perhaps you could find a motel, get some rest and care for your baby," Dr. Randquist informed Isabel.

"We booked a room and had it held so we could check in no matter the time. I'll take the baby there, and I want you to call my cell phone with *any* news. Please!" she pleaded, giving each doctor one of her business cards.

"I promise you'll know as soon as we know, and if surgery is required, we'll try to give you a few minutes to visit prior to his surgery. Is that satisfactory?" Dr. Sweeney vowed.

By this time, I was in a wheelchair. Isabel came to me and said: "Yes, that's fine. Oh, Bill, honey. I love you so much. Please get well, for me and Rebekkah. We need you in our life forever!" She sobbed a little, kissed me, then let me kiss my sleeping daughter.

"I'll be okay. I have my winning team of doctors on the job. I've always had faith in them. I love you, my sweet Isabel, and our darling daughter. I'll see you soon," I promised. An attendant wheeled me down a hallway, and I looked back in time to see Isabel wave at me. I waved back.

The next few hours were tedious. I was poked and prodded to get blood samples and check my responses to different types of stimuli. I was aware when I was put into the MRI chamber, and I thought they were doing it again but in a different machine, which I guessed was the MRA. After that, I lay for a long time in a hospital bed, while the readings were analyzed. I was dozing when I was gently awakened by a nurse. *Déjà vu?*

"Mr. Hollister? Are you awake?" she asked. In my mind, I almost corrected her, saying I was Mr. Lambson.

"Uh, yes. I'm awake. What's up?"

"I was asked to awaken you, so you could be alert, so the doctors could consult with you," she informed me. With that, she left the room and I watched three doctors enter my room: My doctors and a new one.

"Hello, Bill," Dr. Sweeney greeted.

"Hi, guys. What've you found?" I muttered.

"Bill, I was right in thinking you may have an aneurysm," Dr. Randquist informed me.

"So, is there good news to go along with that?" I groaned.

"Well, the good news is we discovered it before it burst and possibly caused your death. But in addition to that, due to your symptoms, we knew we would find it was leaking," Dr. Randquist continued.

"So, what's the rest of it?" I said impatiently.

"The aneurysm is on the right side, in a location difficult to deal with. It *is* operable, but in dealing with the aneurysm, there may be collateral damage to portions of the brain," he continued.

"What kind of damage? Am I going to be a vegetable? An imbecile? A quadriplegic?" I demanded.

"As much as we know about the brain, we don't have it completely mapped, and cannot predict everything possible as an outcome of such surgery. I can only surmise and guess. It may be nothing noticeable; or it could be something catastrophic; or somewhere in between. Dr. Lee, our neurosurgeon colleague, is here and will try to answer your questions. Dr. Lee," Dr. Randquist introduced. The new doctor stepped up to the bed.

"Hello, Mr. Hollister. I'll try to be more forthcoming with a prognosis, given my experience in performing hundreds of this type of surgery. Should I continue, or do you have any immediate questions?" asked Dr. Lee.

"Go ahead, Dr. Lee. Tell me about your experience in these cases," I grumbled.

"I won't say I've dealt with many aneurysms in the location yours is in, but I've done a few. Let me say, there are never aneurysms in ideal locations, where we expect no side effects. The few I have dealt with in the same location have later manifested themselves with such things as slight paralysis of the opposite side of the body the aneurysm is located. Another case caused the patient to have aphasia, which affected their understanding and ability to speak clearly. Still another had recurring seizures, which we were finally able to control with medication. These are worst case scenarios, as I've also had patients with no outward manifestations. We can only be hopeful you fall into the latter group. This is, of course, if you agree to the surgery," he informed me.

"You mean I have a choice? How long would I last, or how far would I get, if I *didn't* have the surgery?" I asked. Dr. Lee deferred to my neurologist.

"Bill, there's no way of telling how long you'd live without some debilitating occurrence. The continued leaking will manifest itself in the same manner it has, thus far: headaches, neckaches, blacking out, or a stroke. At some point, depending on your activities, it could just make you drop dead or worse: let you convulse until you died. Not a pleasant way to go," Dr. Randquist supplied.

"Well, when you put it that way, I have to opt for the surgery. I have too many plans for the future. Does Isabel know yet?" I asked my doctors.

"She knows what we found, but as to the possible side

effects, we thought it best to await her arrival. She's on her way."

"So, how long after the surgery will we know if I'm normal or not?" I queried.

"Recovery will take a few days, in which time we'll constantly evaluate your responses, both mentally and physically... Ah, I see your wife has arrived. Let's bring her up to speed on what we've been discussing," Dr. Sweeney blurted.

I sat in the bed, not so much *stewing*, but I was impatient to get on with it. After half-listening to what they were telling Isabel, she turned to me and came to kiss me.

"Well, my man, you've got yourself into a hell of a mess. I think your doctors believe they can get you out of it, barring any possible side effects," she declared.

"Tell me, doc, do you believe this could have been caused by the lightning strike?" I asked, directing my question to Dr. Randquist.

"Hmm, it's possible, but I doubt it, because I would have expected it to manifest itself within the first couple months, possibly while you were in your, uh, coma," he postulated.

"That's good to know, doc. Well, Izzy, uh, I mean, Isabel, what do you think?" I asked my wife.

Turning to the doctors, she said: "Let's go ahead. I want my husband back, even if I must feed him and change his diapers! No, not really, but I want everything medically possible done, so I can continue to live with and love my hubby; my baby daddy." Isabel sniffled, tears streaming down her cheeks. She then rushed to me and threw herself on my chest.

"Bill, I love you so very much!" she cried. This woke Rebekkah, and she began whimpering. Isabel got off me and attended to our daughter.

The three doctors had probably seen all manner of reactions from patients and family, but they showed they were moved by our emotional outpouring. It was decided surgery would be performed later that very day. They told us I would remain in the hospital for possibly a week or more, depending on what my outcome was from surgery. If required, I'd remain there longer for rehabilitation. Luckily, I was covered by insurance from the university and as a dependent on Isabel's company insurance, which made us feel better about the financial burden of my hospital stay.

Prior to surgery Isabel and I apprised our employers of our situation. I was put on unpaid leave, while Isabel would use PTO for the time she would be here with me. Isabel later told me this: Since we knew no one in town, she stayed at the hospital until after the surgery and recovery period, and then, seeing me still unconscious, she returned to the motel, where she used the time to attempt to do research on her laptop. It was understandably difficult to concentrate. Rebekkah slept through most of it, but occasionally she'd awaken, and Isabel would care for and entertain her.

As for me, I don't remember much. I was aware when they came into my room to shave my head, prepping me for surgery. I hoped Isabel wouldn't be put off by my bald head while I recovered. I was awake when they rolled my gurney into the operating room, which was kept cold. When they transferred me to the operating table, I yelped as the cold stainless steel touched my back and backside. As things began to happen, I was lost in the happenings, and soon Dr. Lee introduced me to my anesthesiologist, who gave me a rundown on what he'd be doing. It was but a moment before I blanked out.

"Bill, can you hear me?" came a soft voice I recognized as Dr. Randquist. I tried to articulate a response, but I choked on something.

"Don't try to talk, Bill. You've been intubated; uh, you have a tube down your throat. Just nod your head if you can understand me," he cautioned. I nodded.

"Good. Can you understand me, clearly? Is your hearing all right?" he continued.

Again, I nodded.

"Great. Now, can you open your eyes?" He asked. With an effort, I pried my eyelids open, as they felt crusty. Finally, I was able to open them fully, and the light of the room shown in, making me squint. Things were blurry at first, but with repeated batting of my eyelids, things cleared, and I saw Dr. Randquist leaning over me.

"That's fine. Can you see me clearly?" He added. I nodded.

"Excellent. Can you move your right arm for me?" he requested. I complied, though I felt stiff.

"Oh, good, good! Now the left, please," he coached. Again, I did so.

"Wonderful!"

Pulling down the bedsheets to uncover my lower limbs, he had me move one then the other of my legs. I felt in control, as far as casual movements went.

"Your EKG and EEG came back normal, so that's a good sign. The incision site should eventually be covered by your hair, if you keep it in the same style you had when you came in. Right now, you look a little rough around the edges, but you'll look much better in a few days. Your wife has been constantly asking when she could see you, and I told her to come to the hospital, hoping you'd respond as you have. She's right outside. Are you ready to see her?" he queried. I nodded.

"Remember, don't try to talk. I'll have someone take you off the ventilator as soon as I can," he replied, walking to the door. In a couple seconds I saw Isabel bring her head into my field of vision.

"Hello, lover boy!" she whispered sexily. I winked at her as seductively as I could manage.

"I'm awfully glad to see you, although you look like you've

been fighting with those bastards again. The doctors are happy, so far, with how things went. It will be a few days before they know for sure if there will be any lasting side effects. I'm pulling for a full recovery, but I'll take you as you are, my sweet husband," she said with tears in her eyes.

At that moment, a respiratory technician came in with a nurse to assist to remove my ventilator. Isabel was asked just to step back. It took but five minutes for them to remove my intubation. They cautioned me that I may have a sore throat and said an attendant would bring in some ice chips. I was catharized, so they could monitor my fluid intake and output. After they left, Isabel was right back at my bedside.

"Where's Rebekkah?" I rasped.

"They have a nice nursery here, and I decided I wanted to see Daddy alone," she replied.

"Oh. How's she been?" I croaked.

"She's been a little angel! She's let me do a lot of work on my doctorate," she bragged.

"How long has it been?" I queried.

"The operation was two days ago in the evening, but they kept you sedated, so you've been out for two nights and one day. This is Saturday morning," she informed me.

"It feels like it's either been an hour or a month," I complained.

"Well, time has no meaning for us since we'll be together for eternity! I love you!" she gushed.

"I hope so, my sweet Isabel. I love you more than I thought possible. What's going to happen? How long are you staying here?" I whispered.

"I plan to drive back tomorrow evening, so I can go into work on Monday. The docs say they want to keep you for at least another week. Dr. Lee watched over you in recovery, then felt you were out of danger and turned you over to Dr. Randquist. Dr. Sweeney has been checking on you too. They seem to have quite the history with you," Isabel commented.

"You have no idea!" I said under my breath.

"What was that?" she quipped.

"I said: you've got that right! They've nursed me through quite a bit," I clucked.

"Yes, they have, and I'm grateful for both times. Imagine never meeting you. I have no idea where I'd be. And don't give me any of your crap about me being with someone better! I know I'm the best I can be with you, my man!" She snapped.

"I'm very happy you think so, my love. I will forever cherish your love," I vowed.

"Now, I should go, so you can get some rest, and be ready for your therapy, which I was told would start this afternoon. Take a long nap, so you'll be raring to go. I love you, sweetie," she advised as she leaned over and kissed me on my lips, despite my suspicions as to the state of my breath.

I couldn't see her walk out in reality, but my mind saw her sashaying like she did in the cafeteria at UTA. I found it almost effortless to fall back to sleep.

I was awakened by a familiar voice. "Well, I'll be damned! Did you come back, just to see me?" My previous physical therapist Roger boomed, as he came into my room.

"I couldn't believe it when I saw your name on my appointment roster. Let me look at your chart, to see how we're going to proceed," he mumbled. Reading through my chart, he hummed a tune I couldn't put a name to, but it was familiar.

"Well, Bill, it looks like you're way ahead of where we began last time I had you as a patient. Today we'll just do a little limbering up exercises right here in bed. We'll make sure you don't show any paralysis in your limbs," he informed. He put me through repeated flexing and movement of all four limbs, massaging the muscles as we went. I grunted and groaned through them all, but his good humor was infectious, and we laughed a lot, my raspy throat notwithstanding. I stopped repeatedly, to take ice chips in my mouth, to keep my throat moist. At the end of the thirty-minute session, he lauded my progress and prophesied he'd have me on the track in no time. I hoped he was right!

Isabel visited me in the evening, bringing Rebekkah with her. Rebekkah was awake and wasn't sure she recognized me with my shaved head, but I tried crooning to her, with my cracking, raspy voice. My soothing tone was recognizable to her, so she soon began her cooing sounds, and as she was used to doing, dropped off to sleep. Isabel was overcome with our interaction since she seldom saw this part of it, as she was studying while this normally occurred.

She beamed at me and said: "Oh, Daddy, you have our daughter enraptured with your lullabies. You should sing to me when we go to bed. Maybe I'll sleep better."

Spending another hour with me, we kept our voices low so Rebekkah could sleep. We talked about inconsequential things, though she did ask me how my therapy had gone, getting a positive report. She said she'd be back the next day at early visiting, so she could be on the road by late afternoon. I warned her about me not getting to brush my teeth yet, but she shushed me and gave me a lip-crushing kiss. Drawing back, she had tears in her eyes.

"Please take care, sweetie. I want to see you home in a week or two. Us girls will see you tomorrow morning. Sleep well, my love," she sighed.

"See you, Izzy! You sleep well too," I whispered. She gathered up the baby carrier and left.

I lay there reviewing my life for the thousandth time. I could not fathom how I was so fortunate to have the life I had, the present situation excluded. Was I happy? Yes, oh yes! Had I succeeded? Well, I had not just 'a' degree, but two. Was I making money, hand-over-fist? No, but I was happy doing what I chose to do, and I was doing all right financially. I had planned out my academic schedule and decided what I wanted to do with my life. I had found a companion I was so much in love with, it hurt to think about it—hurt in a good way! We now had a child, and what could I say about Rebekkah except to say she was perfect? I don't remember having as high an opinion of my first children, though I'm sure they were all exemplary in intellect and work ethic. They were all good in school, including college. No professional athletes, but they all had active, healthy interests in sports: golf, swimming, hiking, and the like. I tried not being biased towards Rebekkah, being so much younger, but my imaginary vest buttons were constantly threatening to pop off.

I realized, then, how different I was as husband and father this second time. As Fred, I had left the nurturing to my wife, and I remained the bread winner and authority figure. I was proud of my first family, but I didn't have the camaraderie with my first wife and children, as I have with Isabel and Rebekkah. I am now *actively* engaged, rather than the *passive* aspect of my involvement with my first family. With a driven effort, I've changed my ways in my professional life and personal one as well.

I loved Isabel and was always anxious to be with her. We're deeply romantic and doted on each other. We showered Rebekkah with love and attention, and as Rebekkah grows older, we'll support her in anything she displays an interest in. It's scary to think about, but if I were to die right then, my only regret would be leaving Isabel without a mate and Rebekkah without a father. Thankfully, I awoke the next morning.

As promised, Isabel and Rebekkah visited me. I'd had the opportunity to brush my teeth by then and wash my face. No hair combing required! Rebekkah was still not sure of me, until I crooned a little to her. She smiled then but wouldn't let Isabel put her in my arms. We visited for a while, then I told

Isabel she should get on the road, so she'd be back in St. Louis by dark. I told her I'd call her if there were any developments, and I'd call her anyway so we could chat. She gave me a *great* kiss and let me give my daughter one, though she struggled to get away from the *scary man*! I watched my loved ones go out my door.

You'd think a patient would get Sunday off, but since I was being evaluated for any side effects of surgery, Roger came to see me and get me out of bed, with all my attendant wires. I didn't have an IV, but they were keeping track of my heart and brain for a few days. With a belt around my waist and holding the monitor, I eased out of bed with Roger's guidance and checked my equilibrium bedside. A little light-headed at first, which I was told was normal, I soon felt balanced, so I started walking around my room, with Roger hovering near me. I couldn't seem to get my left leg to move right. It felt like it was asleep. I mentioned it to Roger, and he sat me back on the bed. Lifting my left leg, he fumbled with something he had in his pocket.

"Can you feel that, Bill?" he asked.

"Feel what? I don't feel anything," I responded, a little alarmed.

"How about this?" he repeated.

"It feels like you're brushing something against my foot," I replied.

"Okay, good. How about this?" he inquired.

"Nothing. Are you touching me?" I asked.

"Sometimes. Just trying some things," he muttered.

"Okay. I want you to *tell* me when you feel something. All right?" he instructed.

For a minute or so, I let him know when I felt him touch me. I couldn't see when or where he was touching me, so I just closed my eyes and concentrated on my sense of touch. Finally, he stood up and looked at me.

"Bill, can you lift your leg?" he asked. I demonstrated the action.

"That's good. At least you're not paralyzed in that leg. It seems you have some spots on your foot and leg which are devoid of feeling. I'll report this to Dr. Randquist and let him evaluate it. For now, though, let's see how much it's going to affect your walking," he suggested.

For the next twenty minutes we walked around my room, then out into the hallway. Roger was right at my side, and occasionally I would stumble a little when my leg seemed to give way. All other exercises Roger had me perform went normally, since I hadn't been bedridden for more than just the last three days and still had all my muscle tone. I was glad I'd been, not so much an *avid* runner, but a *regular* runner.

I was allowed to rest the remainder of Sunday and wondered if Isabel had got off on time. I decided to call her at ten in the evening. She answered after three rings. Her caller I.D. must have come up with the hospital's name, because:

"Hello? Is everything alright with my husband?" came her alarmed response.

"It's me, Izzy. Sorry to alarm you," I apologized. I could hear the relief in her voice.

"Oh, that's okay. It just startled me," she explained.

"Sorry, sweetie. Are you home yet?" I inquired.

"I'm about to enter the city. I should be pulling into the garage in twenty minutes or so. Is everything going all right there?" she asked.

"Sure. They didn't give me Sunday off from therapy, but that was hours ago. I was just lying here, bored, and thought I'd check on my girls. How was the drive?" I babbled.

"The drive was uneventful, except for all the people either returning to St. Louis, or trying the get the heck out of it. Your girls are doing fine. I had to stop a couple time to change our daughter. She does *not* like being wet or messy, and I can't blame her. I can understand why they wouldn't let you lay about on a Sunday, when we're all waiting to see what's happening to your brain and body. By you calling me, I don't have to call you, and I can get Rebekkah into bed, and me too. Didn't they let you keep your cell phone?" she inquired.

"My phone's with my clothes in the closet, but the battery's probably dead, and I don't think I packed my charger. Maybe I can get Roger or one of the attendants to buy me one in the gift shop downstairs," I replied.

"Yes, maybe so," she said distractedly.

"Are you okay, hon?" I fretted.

"Yes. I'm just navigating through traffic. I'm off the freeway now, and we'll be home in no time. Let me go now, but if there's anything happening, call me back, day or night. Okay, my man?" she added.

"Will do. I love you. Give Rebekkah a kiss from Daddy. Night, sweetheart," I ended.

"Goodnight, Daddy. Talk more tomorrow. Bye," she signed off.

During rounds the next morning, Dr. Randquist came in to see me. He had my chart in his hands as he came through the door. As he absorbed what he was reading, I waited for him to address me.

"Hmm, I don't like to see what I'm reading, but there's no real sign of paralysis. Can you get up for me, Bill?" he requested.

As I slid my legs off the bed, he was there to assist me if needed. I stood, a bit shaky, but I recovered soon enough.

"Let's try walking around the room, shall we?" he asked.

Wanting to give him my best efforts, I stepped right out, and as I put my weight on my left leg, I began to fall. Only his assistance prevented me from ending up on my face. After steadying me again, he requested I take smaller steps. My right foot and leg performed great! But about half the time I put my weight on my left foot and leg, I would almost fall. Dr. Randquist helped me back to my bed and had me lie back down.

"What's wrong with me, doc?" I pleaded.

"Bill, I can't say for sure, but with what your physical therapist witnessed, and what I just saw, I suspect you may have *hemiparesis* of the left leg. Normally this is a side effect of a stroke, but since you had some leakage from your aneurysm, it may have caused a mini stroke we didn't detect. What I'm trying to tell you is that you have a slight muscle weakness in your left leg. We didn't see this when you first came out of recovery, because we were looking for paralysis, and since you were able to lift your leg, we thought all was fine. It may pass with continued therapy, but worst-case scenario would be you'll have to walk with a cane, just to add stability and assist you, when the weakness occurs," he instructed.

"So, what do think my chances are, for living a normal life?" I questioned.

"Bill, even if you have to use a cane, occasionally, you'll still be living a normal life. It may even become an affectation, after a while, and you'll think it makes you look sophisticated," he mused.

"You know what I mean. I like to run, for exercise. This would probably end that practice," I groused.

"Let's just see how things go this week. Your therapist will be told what to expect, and we'll see how your therapy goes. By the end of the week, we should have a better perspective for making a prognosis. Okay, Bill?" he enthused.

"Okay, doc. I guess things could be much worse," I admitted.

"That's the spirit. Now, since we're alone, how about telling me about your feelings concerning your *second chance*? We haven't approached the subject for a few months," Dr. Randquist suggested.

"Funny you should ask me about that. I was thinking about that very thing, night before last. I was thinking I was very happy with my life, and if I had died that night, the only regret I would have had, would be leaving my wife and daughter without me around. I want to live forever, if I can stay as happy as I am, though this last bit of news casts a slight pall over things, but it's not a regret. I plan on fully recovering, and if I don't, my wife can tell everyone 'That distinguished man with the cane is my husband!'" I bragged.

"You know, Bill, I'm very pleased to hear that. I am honored to have been a small part of giving you a second chance at life. I'm enheartened to know you were truly committed to doing better with fewer or no regrets. Congratulations. I know Dr. Sweeney feels the same way," he commented.

"I think you and Dr. Sweeney had more than a small part in this. Without you, I would have been food for the worms, and never known such happiness. Thank you," I confessed.

"You're welcome, Bill. Now, I must continue my rounds. I'll leave a note for your therapist. Take care, Bill, and I'll continue to monitor your progress," he concluded.

When Roger came in for therapy, he had read the note Dr. Randquist had left, so we just did a short massage session and then went to the whirlpool to let it further exercise me. After that, he made me walk back to my room with him assisting me. He told me he would find me a cane to use.

I also asked him about a charger for my phone, and he said he'd find one for me. The charger was delivered by a CNA, who told me there were several of them in *lost and found*, left in the rooms by former patients and never reclaimed. I had Roger help me get my phone out of my clothes and plug it into the charger. He also brought me a cane. This would allow me to practice walking on my own. By that night, my phone was charged, so I felt I should call Isabel.

"Is this my baby daddy?" she answered.

"Hi, babe. As you can see, I now have the use of my phone," I informed. "How was your day?"

"Tiring. I wasn't gone long enough for things to take care of themselves, so I played *catch up* on my projects," she groused.

"That's too bad, Izzy. I'm sorry I made you get behind in your work," I apologized.

"Hey, what I did this last week was far more important to me than what I do for the company. I was taking care of my loving husband. Speaking of which, my loving husband, how are things with you? Are you running around the track yet?" she inquired.

"Not quite, though I've been doing a bit of walking," I replied.

"Hmm, are you holding anything back from me, Bill?" she questioned.

"There is a slight glitch with my left leg. It's not paralyzed, but Dr .Randquist thinks I have something called *hemiparesis*. It's weak muscles in my left leg, and I sometimes have it go out on me, so I'm starting to use a cane to walk with. He said I may be able to recover, given further therapy, but no guarantees. Does that make you want to trade me in for a younger model?" I quipped.

"Oh, Bill. I know it bums you, but I keep telling myself it could be much worse. I can buy you a silver handled cane, and you'll be my dashing husband, strutting down the street, pushing Rebekkah in her stroller," she gushed.

"So, you'll take me how I am? That's good, but I'm still going to try to beat this. Hold off on that cane until I see what I can do."

"Of course, I'll take you any way you show up. I love you, Bill, with all my heart," she confessed.

"I love you too, Mrs. Isabel Hollister. How's our baby girl tonight?" I whispered. "She's finally asleep. I think she misses your lullabies. Please hurry back to us. Do you want us to come visit you this weekend?" Isabel revealed.

"Let's see how I do. If there's a chance they'll release me by early next week, things will be okay. I hate to see you driving all that way for just a day or two, and it will take away from your study time. Rebekkah may not like all that time in the car also," I advised.

"So, you don't think they'll release you by Friday?" she said, hopefully.

"With this new wrinkle, I doubt it. But we'll see, and I'll keep you in the loop. As soon as I know, you'll know, even if I have to struggle through a text message," I grumbled.

"But you're getting so much better. I can almost understand what you're telling me," she teased.

"Thanks, Izzy. I appreciate your confidence," I clucked.

"Anytime, lover. Now, I need to use this time to study since I don't have my roommate here to keep tabs on our daughter. I really miss you, Bill," she sobbed.

"I miss you too, my wife. Good luck on your studies, and I'll let you call me tomorrow night if you get the chance. I'm not going anywhere—fast. Love you, sweets! Bye," I commented.

The next day, Roger suggested I go onto the stationary bicycle, so I could exercise my muscles without putting weight on my leg. It was a grueling workout since I hadn't ridden a bike in years. I knew I'd be stiff and sore on Wednesday. I was, but Roger pushed me to repeat the bicycle workout. On Thursday, Roger had me walk around the indoor track using my cane. I still felt weakness in the left leg, though my muscles looked strong. Dr. Randquist and Dr. Sweeney came to see me on Thursday afternoon.

"Bill, your therapist tells us you're really going for the workouts, and that's good, but we don't want you to beat yourself up for not regaining the strength in those leg muscles.

Considering what you're doing, I don't feel we'll see an overnight recovery, and you may never get your full strength back in that left leg. We can keep you here for another week in hopes of a breakthrough, but we feel you'd be better off with your family. You must promise us, though, you'll keep exercising. You could get a stationary bike for home use or get a local gym membership, but above all, keep walking. You can keep the cane we gave you, if you want, or you can get that cane you told me your wife was wanting to get you. What do you think? Are you ready to get out of this place?" Dr. Sweeney asked.

"Frankly, I'm bummed I haven't made more progress, but I understand this type of thing is not a sure thing, cure-wise. I guess I can do just as well at home trying to recover. I know my wife will be glad to get me back there. When will you release me?" I inquired.

"We thought about tomorrow if that's convenient for you. It's safe for you to fly now, or do you want your wife to pick you up?" he questioned.

"I don't mind flying, and it would save her a long drive here and back. Are there any restrictions to keep *me* from driving?" I queried.

"No, unless you have a manual transmission. I don't know how your weakness would affect your operating the clutch," Dr. Randquist answered.

"Yeah, my Subaru does have a clutch. I'll call my wife tonight and see if she wants me to fly or if she'd rather come get me. I'll let you know. Thank you, doctors," I added.

When I figured Izzy would be home, I gave her a call.

"Hi, Izzy. It's just little old me. Are you able to talk?" I stated.

"Hello, my man. I'm just feeding Rebekkah. I can put you on speaker. I know she'd like to hear you voice," she replied. A few seconds later, I could hear background noises, signifying

I was now *on speaker.*

"So, what's happening, baby daddy?" She murmured.

"Well, how anxious are you to have me home?" I teased.

"You're not here, yet?" She giggled.

"That soon, huh? Well, I'm being released tomorrow afternoon, but I wanted to know if you wanted me to fly home or have you drive here to pick me up?" I stated.

"What's the quickest way to see you?" Isabel quipped.

"I guess flying. If you drove here, you'd also have to drive back, as they don't want me driving a car with a clutch," I supplied.

"Oh, so what do they say?" she inquired.

"They say I have to continue to exercise and try to strengthen that leg, but it'd be just as easy to do that at home or a local gym, and I have to keep the cane handy," I muttered.

"Okay. I can pick you up at the airport after I get home from work. I still take public transportation. Do you want me to book your flight?" she asked.

"Sure. Make my departure time around six in the evening to give me time to get from the hospital to the airport. That way, you'll know when to expect me. Thank you, sweet Isabel," I replied.

"Anything to get my man back at home, sweetie. I'll text you the departure time and airline flight number. I can hardly wait to hold you again. You owe me a load of cuddle time, and I plan on collecting soon," she murmured.

"You bet, my love. I'll see you at the airport tomorrow night. Sweet dreams, and give my little girl a kiss for me," I signed off.

On Friday morning, Roger showed up, announcing it would be my last chance to show him what I had, so I let him put me through the *wringer.* I sincerely wanted him to believe he was helping me to recover, and I felt he did. After therapy, I took a breather and then a shower. Being careful never to be too far from my cane, I managed to get dressed and awaited my release. As before, my two doctors and Roger saw me to a cab. Dr. Lee also came to see me off. I was traveling light with no luggage and just what I had in my pockets. They all wished me luck and admonished me to keep in touch. I got another hug from Roger. The cab dropped me off at the airline I had a flight on, and I had over an hour to wait before boarding. While waiting at the gate, I saw a familiar figure sitting by himself. It was my son, Stephen. I debated whether to approach him. He apparently was headed for St. Louis again, unless he had a connecting flight. Walking up to him, he sensed someone approaching and looked up.

"Hello, Mr. Lambson. How are you?" I greeted.

"Uh, Mr., uh, Hollister. How nice to see you again," he responded, noticing my cane. "What brings you to our city, and may I enquire about your infirmity?" he questioned.

"Well, I'm here *because* of my infirmity," I quipped.

"Oh," he returned.

"I was suffering from a brain aneurysm, and the doctors who treated me after the lightning strike wanted me to return so they could take care of me again. I had an operation to repair the aneurysm, and one of the side effects for me was a slight weakness in my left leg, which requires me to occasionally rely on a cane," I supplied.

"Well, I'm sorry to hear about the aneurysm, but I'm also glad to hear you came through with only minor side effects. Please, have a seat. Are you heading back to St. Louis?" he asked.

"Yes, my wife is meeting me at the airport," I added.

"That's very nice for you. Have you been gone from home long?" he queried.

"A week ago yesterday," I commented.

A long silence ensued, as we had made normal small talk, and he once more returned to perusing notes he had pulled up on an electronic tablet. I sat quietly, loathe to interrupt him. When it became time to board our flight, we had seats some distance from each other, so we said our goodbyes and sat down. I felt like I no longer needed to discuss his father. I was content with my life and needed no further validation of my previous one. On deplaning, he was far ahead of me, so I let him go. I had no luggage, and he was headed for the baggage claim.

Isabel met me as I came out of the *arrival gate* and hurried to me with our daughter in her carrier. She didn't care people were gawking at us as she gave me a very warm welcoming kiss and let me kiss our daughter. She found she had to slow her usual rapid gait to my now slower speed. She looked at me apologetically. Once home, I helped her put Rebekkah to bed and stood close by as I crooned her to sleep. All was well with our little world once more. I then had to give Izzy some of her cuddle time, and whatever that led us to. Our weekend was very relaxed, though we both got in some research on our doctorates.

By the time I presented my doctoral dissertation, I was only a couple months behind Isabel. We spent a lot of time teasing each other about 'Doctor' this and 'Doctor' that. Of course, we weren't medical doctors, but Isabel handed me a prescription one evening, with a smoky look in her eyes. It simply read: "Take your wife to bed and practice making a baby. Repeat as necessary." Whatever the doctor ordered! We knew another pregnancy this soon would not make her bosses happy, but by this time she had assistants who could do the hands-on, day-to-day tasks while she kept in loose contact if she went out on a maternity leave of absence. With my PhD, I found a position at Washington University as a Professor of Mathematics.

When Rebekkah was a year old, we decided to move from our condo to a home on acreage in Ladue, an up-and-coming area west of the city. My commute to Washington University was shorter than Isabel's, but not by much. Since we had a good-sized lot, we built a mother-in-law apartment for when Isabel's parents could visit and for any other visitors, such as members of The Gaggle, who infrequently came by.

Life was nice and slow for us, and we took advantage of every relaxing moment. We even found time to support the local firing range, to keep our skill level sharp. I kept in contact with Drs. Sweeney and Randquist, though I had no valuable added information for them, and they kept me informed of any new 'volunteers' for their research. There had been only one other 'transfer,' but it had not been successful, so I remained their *poster child*, though they could hardly publish their success, due to the poor ramifications. Granted, I had volunteered for it, but you can imagine the reactions from the Lambsons and the medical profession in general. It felt like finding the equivalent to the Fountain of Youth but not being able to tell anyone where it is. The ethical questions alone could destroy their careers.

I had agonized since the very beginning whether I should try to tell Isabel about it all, but I was scared to death of what her reaction would be. Would she think me demented, or perhaps she would believe me but be abhorred about being with such an old man. Best to keep mum still. I thoroughly enjoyed teaching, and some of my math students were very promising. I had some return to the university to tell me how much they appreciated my presentations, in which they found a true love of mathematics, and some even said they thought about teaching at some level. It was very gratifying to me. I still used a cane but had adjusted to using it. At the same time, Isabel was an invaluable engineer with seemingly unlimited potential.

We had a visit from Isabel's parents, and though we were reluctant, we let our precious Rebekkah, now nearly two, go back with them to Florida to spend a week. During that week, Isabel and I tried to enjoy our solitude, but understandably, we felt the void. As we sat on our back veranda in the cool of the evening, we reminisced about our life together. There were many poignant moments, and we shed a few tears recalling memories, but there were also funny remembrances, so we laughed too! I had come to a decision and waited for the right moment.

I took her hand and said: "Do you remember, when we'd known each other for only a short time, and I made some comment that I don't remember, but you said something about me seeming older than I was?"

"Yes. I vaguely remember because your phrasing was like how an older person would have expressed it," she recalled.

"So, what would you say if I told you I was really eighty instead of thirty-something?" I ventured.

"I'd say: Don't try to pull that *old man* crap on me. Rebekkah is being taken care of for a week, so I want you to take me inside, and we can continue to reminisce by you showing me how much you still love me after all these years!"

Well, so much for trying to be truthful. So, I just did what the doctor ordered. Second chances are wonderful! And I wouldn't change this one for two or three more.

About Atmosphere Press

Atmosphere Press is an independent, full-service publisher for excellent books in all genres and for all audiences. Learn more about what we do at atmospherepress.com.

We encourage you to check out some of Atmosphere's latest releases, which are available at Amazon.com and via order from your local bookstore:

Dancing with David, a novel by Siegfried Johnson

The Friendship Quilts, a novel by June Calender

My Significant Nobody, a novel by Stevie D. Parker

Nine Days, a novel by Judy Lannon

Shadows of Robust, a novel by K. E. Maroudas

Home Within a Landscape, a novel by Alexey L. Kovalev

Motherhood, a novel by Siamak Vakili

Death, The Pharmacist, a novel by D. Ike Horst

Mystery of the Lost Years, a novel by Bobby J. Bixler

Bone Deep Bonds, a novel by B. G. Arnold

Terriers in the Jungle, a novel by Georja Umano

Into the Emerald Dream, a novel by Autumn Allen

His Name Was Ellis, a novel by Joseph Libonati

The Cup, a novel by D. P. Hardwick

The Empathy Academy, a novel by Dustin Grinnell

Tholocco's Wake, a novel by W. W. VanOverbeke

Dying to Live, a novel by Barbara Macpherson Reyelts

Looking for Lawson, a novel by Mark Kirby

Surrogate Colony, a novel by Boshra Rasti

Orleans Parish, a novel by Chad Pentler

The Gift of Dragons, a novel by Rachel A. Greco

About the Author

Having completed three separate careers: military, industry, and healthcare, the author has traveled widely and is an avid reader. His interests include: history, music and art, in no particular order. In addition to this story, he's created others, and several poems. He continues to write daily and looks forward to publication of his other works. The author is married, with adult children and grandchildren from pre-teen to young adult. He is a self-professed romantic, and his other works contain romantic threads running through his story-lines.

CPSIA information can be obtained
at www.ICGtesting.com
Printed in the USA
LVHW031511180522
719025LV00005B/189